dangerous attraction

ANASTASI FAMILY SYNDICATE

DORI PULITANO

BEHIND THE BADGE PRESS

acknowledgments

Dear Readers,

First off, thank you for ourchasubf this book. The *Anastasi Family Syndicate* holds a special place in my heart because each character's name was plucked right off my family tree. Before my mother passed away, she was knee-deep in genealogical research. So, all the names in this story are tied to my lineage—name only, of course; the rest is pure fiction. Or is it?

This special edition is a re-release of the series, now with added sparkle. Each book has been re-edited to include new content. While the characters remain the same, some of the storylines have had a facelift. I hope you love it even more than the first version!

This re-release wouldn't have seen the light of day without a few amazing people. So, a big thank you to:

My husband for pushing me to take a leap of faith and create something beautiful. I was scared sh*tless, but he was brave enough for both of us.

Sara, for enduring my near mental breakdowns and not dumping me as a friend. You put up with my bullsh*t and stayed by my side as I worked through the kinks of this story.

LeeAnn, for always being there when I needed you and making me feel important. Life would be colorless without you, and since I prefer things in technicolor, I'm keeping you around.

Without these folks, this book would still be basic.

And finally, to you, the readers. Because without readers, the writer only wastes their words. Don't let mine go to waste.

Dori

family tree

Giuseppe Anastasi & Vittoria Anastasi
Grandfather/Deceased & Grandmother

Giacomo Anastasi
Godfather of Syndicate

Giorga Anastasi
Giacomo's Wife

Massimo Anastasi
28 years old
Don/Capo Famiglia
7-7-1996
Velvet Ace Lounge & Casino

Madison Heart
20 years old
College Student
4-31-2004

Vincenzo Anastasi
26 years old
Underboss
5-18-1998
The Sapphire Dagger

Antonio Anastasi
24 years old
Captain/Caporegime
11-3-1999
Emerald Ace
Holdings

Catarina Anastasi
26 years old
ER Nurse
8-9-1997

FAMILY TREE

Celestina Anastasi
21 years old
College Student
10-1-2002

Carmela Anastasi
21 years old
College Student
10-1-2002

notable characters

Donny Cesare Russo
Consigliere/Capo

Alex Coulter
Former Detective/Head of Security at Velvet Ace

Drew Mancini
Enforcer

Carlisle Casteneli
Manager/Bartender Velvet Ace

Harley Cook
Nurse

Miguel Angel
Sureños Leader

Kevin Luchasi
Anastasi Family Doctor

Manuel Costa
Javier's Brother

Cristian Silva
Chilean Mafia Underboss

Javier Costa
Sureños Former Leader

Matias Silva
Head of Chilean Mafia

Bastian Silva
Chilean Mafia Captain/Caporegime

Filippo Bianchi
Godfather Rome Italy Mafia

Sofia Bianchi
Underboss Reno Mafia

Bruno Stepanov
Russian Mob

Lorenzo Bianchi
Don Reno Mafia

Aleski Lipovsky
Russian Mob Leader

Andrei Sloski
Russian Mob

series reading order

DANGEROUS ATTRACTION

MASSIMO & MADISON'S BOOK

DARK DESIRE

VINCENZO & RILEY'S BOOK

FATAL LOVE

ANTONIO, MIA & MICHAEL'S BOOK

DEADLY INTENTIONS

CATARINA & DONNY'S BOOK

CARNAGE HEART (NOVELLA)

BECKETT'S STORY

SAVAGE HEARTS

CELESTINA & BECKETT'S STORY

FRACTURED DEVOTION

CARMELLA & ALEX'S BOOK

Grab the entire series on E-Book at
https://alphabookboyfriends.com/collections/bundles/bundles

reader warning

Like most Mafia books, this series contains scenes that may be difficult for some to handle. Human trafficking, violence, male/male/female romance, kidnapping, and attempted suicide are addressed throughout the six-book series.

If that is not something you can handle, please discontinue reading.

Suicide is a serious matter. If you or anyone you know in the United States is contemplating suicide, please seek help by reaching out to Lifeline at https://988lifeline.org/ or by dialing 988 from your phone. International assistance is available by visiting https://blog.opencounseling.com/suicide-hotlines/

More than 27 million people around the world endure the abhorrent abuse of human trafficking and forced labor, including thousands of people right here in the United States. It is a threat to global security, public safety, and human dignity. If you believe you are a victim of human trafficking or may have information about a potential trafficking situation, don't hesitate to get in touch with the U.S. National Human Trafficking Hotline at https://humantraffickinghotline.org/. If you or someone you know is in immediate danger, please call 911.

I never lie to any man because I don't fear anyone. The only time you lie is when you are afraid.

John Gotti

one

MASSIMO

THERE ARE moments in life that define *you*.

Moments that make *you*.

Moments that shape you into the person you will inevitably become until your death.

This was *not* that moment.

No…this was my job—a job I'd been born into.

"Did you hear what I asked you?" I gripped the man's portly neck, my hand itching to snap his spine like a twig.

Sweat trickled down his head, seeping into the rolls of skin beneath my fingers, digging into his flesh. I yanked his head back, forcing him to look into my eyes. The piece of shit stole from me, and that wasn't going to fly—no one stole from the Anastasis and lived to brag about it… Especially someone who worked for me. The funny part is this dumb mother-fucker thought no one would notice the missing money or guns, but a hundred grand and an entire shipment of assault rifles just doesn't up and walk away without being seen.

The missing money and guns was deliberate, and this fucker had the balls to think he could pull a fast one on me. What he didn't expect was I didn't miss a thing when it came to the club. I felt the rage bubbling up, and I knew I had to make an example out of whoever stole from me.

That's how we ended up in this dimly lit basement, where the air was thick with the stench of fear and desperation. I wanted him to feel every ounce of my wrath. I leaned in closer, my voice a low growl. "You really thought you could steal from me? From my family?" His eyes widened with terror, his lips trembling as he tried to form words, but nothing coherent came out.

"You think you're smart, huh?" I sneered. "Thought you could just take what's mine and walk away?" His pathetic whimpers were music to my ears. This wasn't just punishment; it was a lesson to anyone else who might get any ideas. Stealing from me was a death sentence, plain and simple.

My fingers tightened on reflex as I leaned into him, demanding answers. "Where is the money, Franklin?" I knew before he spoke he wasn't going to give me what I wanted.

He sobbed, and his face was coated in a sheen of snot. "Please, Mr. Anastasi… I didn't mean for things to get so out of hand. I was desperate and let my stupidity get me here." He pressed his hands together like he was praying. "Surely you can let me fix this. I've worked for your family for a long time." His voice hitched as he tried to plead for his life. "I made a mistake."

"A mistake?" A manic laugh escaped my lips as I glanced over at my head enforcer. "A mistake is shorting the till twenty bucks. But taking a hundred grand *and* losing a shipment of guns? That's no fucking mistake."

I released his head, then dusted my palms on my pants. Not only was I stuck dealing with his sorry ass, but I was also doing it in my favorite suit. Franklin had been in charge of our books at the shipping yard for the last six years. But unbeknownst to us, he'd been slowly skimming money off the top—money that was going somewhere else. When I got word a shipment of guns had gone missing, I began to dig. That's when I found the discrepancy in the money—and the trail led straight to him.

"Donny." I turned to the muscle of my operation. "Let's show him what happens when someone betrays the family."

"No…please… I have a family."

I watched as Donny slipped the cigar cutter from his pocket. "Franklin, you should have thought about your family before you stole from me. Last chance to tell me who you took the money for and where the shipment went. We know you're involved. There's no sense in denying it. Save yourself the agony, and just tell me what I want to know." I gave him enough time to take a breath before nodding to Donny. Pulling his hand straight, Donny slipped the circular blade over his digit and clamped down. Blood spurted out, and droplets splattered against my cheek while Franklin screamed in agony. "I can keep going all night, Franklin… Where. Is. The. Money?"

"He'll kill me."

Smirking, I lifted my eyes to Donny's. "He's worried about someone else killing him." I huffed a laugh as I slipped my jacket off. After tossing it on the table beside me, I removed my cufflinks and shoved them in my pocket. There was no way I was going to let this pig's blood ruin a five-thousand-dollar pair of links. It was bad enough I was subjecting the expensive fabric of my suit to his disgusting sweat. Slowly, I rolled my sleeves up before slamming my fist into his face, making his head snap back in the chair. "You should be worried about me," I said.

Donny leaned into him as he clipped another finger off. "You ready to talk, or should I have him move on to something else more painful? Actually, we should call Vincenzo in—he'd get off on this."

"No..." The threat of my brother, who is known in our circle for his ruthlessness, sends the grown-ass man into a fit of sobs. "Please, not La Lama—anything but him. I beg you."

I closed my eyes and took a deep breath. I had no intention of calling Vincenzo to deal with this low-level piece of shit. Vin didn't deal with this part of the family anymore, but I wasn't going to tell this fuckface that. Letting him believe my brother was coming to filet his skin was good enough.

"We're not getting anywhere, Franklin. You've wasted my money, and now you're wasting my time."

Time was money, and standing there arguing with a man who'd already taken enough of both from me was pointless—adding in my brother would be an even bigger waste. It was obvious this asshole wasn't going to give up who he'd been working for. I slipped my gun from the leather beneath my arm and pressed the barrel against his head.

"I hope the money was worth your life." The sound of the gun going off echoed into the room as his head exploded across the concrete floor.

I glanced at Vito, one of my men who'd been observing the interaction from the corner and spoke. "Vito, come help Donny dump his ass." I stepped back, pulled a handkerchief from my pocket, and wiped the remnants of his betrayal from my skin. "Let me know when this is done. Someone else was involved, and we'll flush out the other traitors soon. In the meantime, I need you to make sure a statement is made with this piece of shit's corpse."

I watched as Donny stepped forward and rolled up his sleeves. Usually, I would take my time teaching those who stole from my family a lesson, but the thought of ruining my suit pissed me off.

The door slammed shut behind me as I strode from the room, leaving my men to clean up the betrayal left behind by the massive door, keeping the family secrets hidden from the unsuspecting patrons upstairs. As the son of Giacomo Anastasi, Don of one of the longest-running crime families in Vegas, I couldn't let anyone see me as weak. Especially a man who I trusted to work for me. I couldn't let others think it was okay to take from us. So, sending a message was imperative—it was our way of life.

The mafia was deeply ingrained in my blood.

I slipped my phone out of my pocket and fired off a text to my father—the Don.

It's done.

My father moved to Vegas from Sicily at my grandfather's request. After a visit to the States, my grandfather wanted to control the streets of Vegas, and he did that by helping to establish my father's place. It was a long road, but the Anastasis had become a name everyone feared. Even the morally bound protectors of our fine city were in our pocket. We had our finger on the pulse of Vegas, leaving nothing to chance when it came to our business dealings. And if, by some off chance, we didn't know, someone learned quickly why keeping secrets wasn't in their best interest.

From a young age, I knew being the oldest meant I had a very specific duty to the family. A duty which left little time for anything that wasn't in the best interest of the family—like dealing with men who betray us. My father also expected me to oversee the operations of our family's businesses—the Velvet Ace Lounge and Casino being one of them.

When I turned eighteen and took my place beside my father, I added a few things to the casino—perks that benefited the patrons and, more importantly, my family. I converted part of the casino to offer secluded rooms with bar service for more private meetings. The services offered ranged from high-stakes poker games to more… personal entertainment. They were mainly used by high-profile customers who wanted to be away from the public eye so they could let go of pretenses. When people felt comfortable in their environment, they tended to have loose lips.

This boded well for business—well, *my* business now. A month ago, I took over as Don in Vegas. My grandfather's health had been steadily declining, which meant my parents had to go back to their homeland so my father could take over as the head of the family there—which left Vegas to me.

Managing the Velvet Ace Lounge and Casino wasn't just about running a business; it was about maintaining a strategic advantage. The information gathered in our establishment was invaluable. Politicians, celebrities, and influential businessmen all frequented our casino, and when they let their guard down, they became an open book. We had files on everyone, and we had leverage whenever we needed it.

After ensuring the basement door was secured, I headed into the club. It was a typical Friday night, with people crowded inside and dressed to impress. Everyone was out looking for something, and often, they found it at our place. The dim lighting and pulsating music created an atmosphere that was both exciting and unnerving.

"Carlisle," I called out, weaving through the throng of people until I reached the bar. My voice carried a hint of weariness, a byproduct of the day's endless demands. I furrowed my brows when I noticed Julie, one of my long-standing servers, behind the bar with him. She typically worked in the private rooms, so seeing her at the bar raised my hackles. "Who's working the room if she's out here?"

"Brian. Julie has been filling in for Kitty since she quit, but she isn't happy about it," Carlisle said, his tone tinged with frustration as he glanced back at Julie.

I tapped the bar top. "So hire someone else. We can afford it, trust me."

The club was a money maker—not to mention it was one of many covers for the actual cash cow, our arms dealing. My dad had decided early on we would sell guns only. He despised drugs and anything to do with the sex trade. So, while we didn't deal with drugs directly, we controlled who did.

Carlisle shook his head. "I've tried. Trust me, but the expectations leave the options limited."

I sighed a deep, resigned breath. The club was often a source of stress on top of the other issues I dealt with for the family. Having been with me for the last five years, Carlisle knew what I expected when it came to the people I employed. "It shouldn't be that difficult to find someone who isn't a hooker. Surely you can find a woman who is looking for work and not a quick fuck with me or my brothers."

"You'd think. But most of the women who've applied should be sending their *résumés* to the titty bar, not here. There was one girl, but she's not the usual type we employ."

"What do you mean—not our usual type?"

Carlisle shrugged. "For one, she's a college student."

"Bring her in after you do a background. If she's the only one standing out among the bimbos you're telling me applied, what can go wrong? Once you do the interview, I'll meet with her and make the final decision."

"You got it," Carlisle said, then moved to the opposite end of the bar to serve a couple of guys.

Glancing around, I smiled, knowing I'd helped make the casino what it had become. The lower-level bar and dance floors were still the main attraction, but I renovated them by adding two additional floors. The basement continued to be used for meetings we needed to keep out of the public's eye —a space for us to discuss things that pertained to our morally gray activities. By adding to the Black Ace Lounge, we had an environment that provided unfiltered access to information from some of the city's most high-ranking officials—a blackmail of sorts.

The best addition, however, was Onyx on the second floor. That part of the club was a members-only accessible area. Anyone wanting to partake in the services offered at Onyx had to pay a hefty club membership and sign the required non-disclosure form, which kept the activity of the members private. Politicians didn't want their constituents to learn they had a Daddy kink, for example, and the exclusivity of the club meant no one could use information gained during their time in the club for their own benefit.

Well…*except* for us.

The bartenders knew how to mix drinks strong enough to lower inhibitions, but not so strong that they'd forget the night's events. On the surface, the Velvet Ace was a popular place for people to dance, drink, and win some money. But beneath that façade, it was a carefully constructed web of information and influence all serving my family.

That meant I had to keep my finger on the pulse of my employees. I took care of them, and in return, they turned their cheek the other way when we needed to deal with things outside the law without asking questions or being told. I slid from my stool and downed the remaining amber liquid. I was too keyed up to go home—the stress of the day weighed heavily on my shoulders.

I needed to go blow off some steam… a willing, tight body was exactly what I craved.

MASSIMO

I'D BARELY MADE it to the elevator to Onyx, where I'd find a willing participant in my need to destress, when a scantily dressed woman stepped into my path. Her perfume was overpowering, a heavy sweetness that made my nose twitch.

Right now, women were only good for one thing—sex. Until I could find a woman who could handle being part of my world, using them for their body was all I sought. Most of the women I found in The Velvet Ace were after money or fame —neither of which was befitting of my future wife...a woman who'd be my queen.

The club allowed me the opportunity to get my rocks off without attachment—something I avoided at all costs. I didn't have time to search for the *right* one, not when I was next in line to take over our family's empire. I could only hope she'd find me instead. If I was going to be the king one day, I needed someone who understood her role beside me—these women were far too plastic and would break under the pressures of being an Anastasi. So easy was something I needed for the time being—and looking at the woman standing in front of me, I knew she'd serve my needs for the night. Plus, she had a decent pair of tits.

"Where are you going all alone?" she whispered in a seductive voice, her breath warm against my neck. She stuck out her bottom lip in a pout, her eyes widening in a faux display of disappointment. "I was watching you at the bar and was hoping you'd notice me."

Glancing over her decent body, I forced myself to seem more interested than I was. I only wanted her for one thing. I didn't care about the small talk. "I was wrapped up in more important business."

"Wouldn't you rather be wrapped up in me?" Her hand slid down the front of my shirt and rested at the top of my belt, where her fingers lingered close to my zipper with a silent promise. I grabbed her wrist, applying pressure to halt her wandering hands. Where did she get off touching me like that? I was in no mood.

This woman was just another gold digger hoping to gain bragging rights for sleeping with an Anastasi. Usually, I'd walk away, but she wasn't hard on the eyes, and I needed my dick sucked. Her long brown hair hung loosely around her shoulders, and she was wearing a tube-style dress that barely covered her tits or ass. While she was pretty, she didn't get my body humming like I wanted—but I was too tired to hunt for something better.

"Is that so? Do you usually make it a point to proposition men?" I wasn't about to get twisted up with a hooker, not when I could get pussy for free. And despite the tight security, they still made it through the long lines to get inside. I didn't care for the used-up pussy in my casino, but my patrons, who couldn't pick up a woman, liked having options. It wasn't my place to dictate who they fucked—I just didn't let it into my private club upstairs. That was for consenting partners who craved a kinky lifestyle.

"Only the ones who look like they could use a distraction." I forcefully made her grab my cock, causing her to purr. "You have my panties soaked."

She grabbed my hand and pushed it between her thighs. True to her word, the thong she had on was soaked through. Rubbing my fingers across the lace, I snatched at the flimsy fabric and ripped it off her body. My fingers pinched the swollen bud, drawing a gasp from her lips. Women knew who I was, and they all tried to capture my attention. And while I'd fucked my fair share, none of them got more than my cock for a night.

Gripping the woman's wrist in my hand, I tugged her against my chest, my other fingers still covering her pussy. "Think you can handle what I need?"

"I can take it," she panted as she ground her body against mine.

Pulling my hand from beneath her dress, I tugged her back toward the dance floor.

"I thought we were going to your place?"

"I don't take women to my place. Wait here," I ordered, leaving her standing by the bank of elevators I was initially taking to Onyx. Looking at this girl, I didn't want to give her the impression she was important—she wasn't.

"Follow me," I grabbed her elbow and drug her through the throng of people. She struggled to keep up in the ridiculous heels she had on, but I didn't care. We weaved through the crowd and past the dance floor, where bodies moved in a rhythmic, almost primal dance. The air was thick with sweat and pheromones, a heady mix that made my pulse quicken. "You sure you want this?"

She leaned into me, reached around, and palmed my cock again. Squeezing it through the fabric of my pants, "Yes." She smiled up from beneath her lashes, her eyes hooded with lust.

We'd barely made it into the hallway before I was pressing her against the wall. I growled, my want to dominate almost overpowering. "You'll do everything I say—and don't get it in your head that this is more than exactly what this is–you sucking my cock.. Strip your dress off." There was suddenly an intense need to relieve the pressure building inside my dick.

"Here?" She looked down the hallway toward the mass of people on the dance floor.

"No one cares. I thought you said you could handle what I needed?" I cocked an eyebrow at her, daring her to defy me.

Hooking her fingers in the stretchy fabric, she slid her dress down below her tits. Her voluptuous breasts popped out to show her already hard nipples. Her dress was bunched around her middle, exposing her pussy to everyone. I stepped around her and started toward my office, forcing her to walk through the empty hall nearly naked. It was cruel, but I had to remain in control. This was just about getting off, and she needed to remember she was a means to an end—nothing more.

She started to tug her dress back up, but I grabbed the material and shoved it back down. "Don't cover yourself. Let them see who I'm about to fuck."

She stood tall as she walked through the corridor, not flinching as several men glanced her way before realizing she was with me. They nodded in approval as I grabbed her hand and shoved her inside. My office was dimly lit by the soft glow of lamps that cast shadows on the dark walls. A large leather couch dominated one side, and a massive wooden desk filled the remaining space.

"I'm in control." Slipping off my jacket, I slowly rolled my sleeves up to my forearms and stepped closer to her body. "Do you understand?" She nodded. "I need words."

She bit her lip and grinned. "Yes, I understand."

"Good. Get on your knees and take out my cock."

She slid to the floor and slowly opened my pants. Her fingers grazed my erection as she lowered the zipper. I stifled a laugh when she shuddered at the realization I was not your average guy. I was proud of my dick—all ten inches—and had earned a reputation for it among the ladies. She slipped her hand into my boxers and tugged my length out.

"Oh…" She whimpered as she began to stroke me.

I fisted her hair, jerking her head to look me in the face. "Are you going to be able to take all of me? Spit on it if you need to."

Without saying a word, she leaned forward and took me into her mouth. I knew she wouldn't be able to swallow all of my cock, but I flexed my hips, shoving as many inches as I could into her throat. The force of my thrust caused her to gag. Grabbing my legs, she steadied herself before moving her head in a messy rhythm. I grabbed her hair tight, guiding her face back and forth as I fucked her mouth. Pounding away as she held onto my thighs, I pushed toward my release. Not finding the relief I needed, I fisted her hair and pulled her from around my cock. As much as I wanted to cum, she wasn't doing it for me with her mouth.

"Jack me off."

Her tiny hands wrapped around my girth. She couldn't just use one hand, so she used both to create a steady pace along my shaft. Closing my eyes, I let my mind wander to the woman on her knees. She held onto my cock and flicked her tongue against my crown, her breasts bouncing as she jerked me to release.

"Fuck." I grunted as my orgasm rippled through my body.

Hot streams of cum spurted onto her chest, covering the bunched material gathered around her middle in a sticky mess as my shaft jerked in her hand. My dick softened against my leg as I stepped out of her hold, forcing her to let go of my shaft.

"Get up and get your clothes on." I stalked toward my desk, shoving myself back into my pants.

She wobbled toward me on her heels, her eyes wide with desperation. "What about me?" she whispered, her voice trembling.

I didn't even pause to consider her plea. I turned around and grabbed her arm with a grip that made her wince. "This wasn't for you," I said coldly, not bothering to mask the disdain in my voice. Without a second thought, I dragged her to the door and yanked it open. "Get out, and don't fucking come looking for me again."

"But..." she started, her voice barely more than a breath. I didn't let her finish. I tossed her away from me with a force that sent her stumbling. She collided with the doorframe, her eyes wide with shock. Without another glance, I slammed the wooden barrier in her stunned face.

She was a means to an end. Nothing more. I felt no remorse, no guilt. If anything, I was left even more frustrated than before. Rubbing the bridge of my nose, I slid into the chair behind my desk, my mind already shifting away from her and back to more pressing matters.

three

MASSIMO

SOMETHING about the interaction with Franklin still left me on edge. How had an employee betrayed us so easily? The uncertainty and the sense of danger lurking just out of sight gnawed at me.

I grabbed the phone from its perch on my desk and dialed my brother. The tension in my muscles refused to dissipate as I waited for him to answer.

"Fratello," I said as soon as he picked up, leaning back and placing my elbows on the desk. My mind raced with possibilities, each one more troubling than the last. I flipped the signature black playing card I carried everywhere between my fingers. "I need you to come to the club in the morning."

Antonio didn't ask why. He never did. "I'll be there," he replied, his voice steady.

I hung up the phone and stared at the playing card in my hand. I couldn't afford to show weakness, not now, not ever. The stakes were too high, and the game was far from over.

My brother sat across from me, a mask of concern marring his face. At twenty-four, and the youngest son, Antonio, wore his emotions on the surface. And right now, he was a mixture of anger and worry. His normal jokester personality was missing as he listened to Donny speak.

"We left Franklin's family a clear understanding of what happens when you betray the family—but we still don't know why he took the money or where the guns went."

"I think I might have an idea about that." Antonio blew out a breath. "The driver of that rig was found dead." He cut his eyes toward me. "I got the call late last night."

"Fuck." I threw the card down on the desk. "Who was with him?"

"Jose Juarez." He flipped his phone around and slid it across the desk. "And about twenty minutes ago, I got this."

I glanced down at the screen and read the text that had my brother in knots. "What the fuck?"

Handing Donny the phone, I said, "I need you to get Alec on this."

"Someone has some big balls, boss." Donny grunted. "But this definitely points to Jose being involved."

"That motherfucker is definitely involved." My brother pushed to his feet. "The picture of our tractor-trailer might not say, 'hey, we stole your guns,' but it's a pretty big indicator. Hell, whoever sent it thanked me personally for the shipment being on time. You know as well as I do I haven't made any other *deliveries*."

The ringing of my phone halted the conversation. "What?" I snapped into the line, "Right now? Fine. Send her in." Donny's brows raised as he waited for me to explain. "Donny, go with Antonio. You two go pay Juarez's family a visit and see if they know where he is." I leaned back in my chair. "Then find that bastard and bring him in."

Donny nodded in acquiescence. Getting his hands dirty was part of his job as the muscle of my operation.

Antonio stood. "Does Dad know?"

"Not yet, but as soon as I'm done with this interview, I'll call him. Not much he can do from Sicily."

Antonio grunted, "And Vincenzo?"

I waved my hand through the air. "I'll fill him in later." Vincenzo, the second oldest, handled the money laundering aspect of our organization through his restaurant, The Sapphire Dagger. The dark corners of our lives left scars, some visible, some not, and Vincenzo had his share—which meant I only brought him in on things when it was absolutely needed. Right now, calling him would do nothing more than trigger a past he was desperately trying to forget. A past I nearly lost him to completely.

A tap at the door interrupted us. Antonio pulled open the barrier to let Carlisle step through. Antonio jerked his head at me. "We'll see you later." I watched as he stepped into the hall, followed by Donny.

"Well, hello there, beautiful."

I heard Antonio mutter the words to someone in the hallway out of view. I sat up in my chair at the sudden change in my brother's behavior. Antonio was the flirt in the family, and whoever was standing with Carlisle had piqued his interest.

Carlisle's deep voice echoed through the office. "Mr. Anastasi, your interview is here."

"Send her in."

Carlisle stepped to the door and motioned to whoever was hiding out of view. Nothing could have prepared me for the woman who walked in behind him. Sure, I'd read her file and seen the headshot Alec had pulled from the college server. But *fuck*…the student identification had done her no service. She was stunning.

Her chestnut brown hair was pulled into a sleek ponytail, begging for me to reach up and tug it free. The blue of her irises held me hostage, sending a bolt of lust straight to my cock. Shifting in my seat, I smiled. Her crystal blue orbs held a mix of wonder and fear as she stood there.

"Sir, this is Madison Heart." Carlisle waved her further inside. "I'll leave you two alone. Let me know when you're done, and I'll come escort her out, sir."

Dismissing him with a flick of my wrist, I watched Madison fidget in place. This girl was terrified, something that left me with a strange mix of emotions. "Please. Have a seat."

I motioned to the chair across from me. When she didn't move, I realized she was obviously stuck in her head. I could sense the nervous energy beneath her composed exterior. I leaned back in my chair, studying her. "So, Madison. Tell me why you want to work for me."

"This job is a great opportunity," she replied, trying to keep her voice steady. "I've heard a lot about your casino and its reputation."

I could only imagine what she'd heard. Looking at her file, I noted she'd lived in Las Vegas her whole life, some of which was in foster care. "I see. And what exactly have you heard?"

"Um…" She bit down on her lip before answering. "Just that you have high expectations, and you pay your employees well."

"Both true. I demand the best out of the people I employ. I also expect loyalty from everyone I pay—which is well above the average casino. But why here? Why not apply to one of my other businesses? Surely, you know this isn't the only place my family owns. The casino seems a bit—odd for a girl coming from somewhere like Gino's Pizzeria."

"I believe I can bring a lot of energy and dedication to your team. Plus, I've got experience as a server, as you obviously know. I can give you Gino's number if you need a reference."

"Sweetheart," I lean forward across my desk, "I owned Gino's." Madison's face turned pale as the words sank in; her wide, open eyes locked onto mine in utter disbelief. Her eyebrows shot up, while her mouth fell open, frozen in a silent gasp. The shock on her face was amusing. "Yes, I'm aware your previous place of employment burned down. But that's not the only restaurant in town."

A local gang had torched Gino's in retaliation for us not letting them peddle their drugs. Fortunately, no one had been hurt, but the business was a total loss.

She looked down at her hands in her lap. "Gino's was the only one willing to accommodate my school schedule."

"What makes you think I'll accommodate your class schedule?"

My smartass tone made her head snap up. I smirked as I watched her eyes widen a fraction before she schooled her expression. "I don't. But after applying nearly everywhere else, I took a chance."

Leaning back in my seat, I studied her. This woman had curves in all the right spots—the kind that made a man's cock stand at attention and take notice. She was wearing a pair of tennis shoes that added to the absurdness of a girl like her sitting in my casino. My eyes traveled up her body, tracing the line of her neck and settling on her gaze again. Her face was the perfect shape, with the most kissable full lips I'd seen in a while. They had me imagining her mouth wrapped around my shaft. Shifting myself, I continued my appraisal of her. This beautiful specimen had alabaster skin dusted with the perfect number of freckles. Freckles, I itched to count while she was naked.

Shaking myself out of the dirty thoughts I was having, I cleared my throat. "I don't think you're the type of woman we need here."

"Please… I promise I might look like a far cry from the beautiful women I saw out there when I came in, but I can handle it. I've grown accustomed to getting just a few hours of sleep. School won't interfere with my job if that's what you're worried about." She gave me a timid smile.

"I'm not worried about that." I sighed.

Madison shifted in her chair and leaned forward. "Look, I need this job. My scholarship isn't covering my living expenses. I'm on the verge of losing my apartment, and that can't happen."

Watching her body language, I knew she was serious. The thought of this woman struggling made something inside me coil with anger. My protective needs rose again, but this time, I wanted to throw her over my shoulder and lock her away from the harsh world that was ready to chew her up and spit her out.

I scrubbed my palm down my face. I didn't know this girl. Caring about someone's welfare outside the family wasn't something I usually took an interest in, but something about her had me wanting to throw all my old beliefs out the window.

I nodded slowly, never taking my eyes off her. "All right, Miss Heart. I'll give you a trial run tonight."

"Tonight?" she sat up in her chair. Relief washed over her face, mixed with lingering anxiety. "Thank you, Mr. Anastasi. I won't let you down."

"Be here tonight at eight. We'll see how it goes." Leaning forward, I narrowed my gaze at her. "If all goes well, I'll bring you on part-time. We'll let Carlisle know your schedule since he's the person you'll report to directly. The starting pay for the position is thirty thousand. We also provide employee benefits after thirty days."

Madison choked on a gasp. "Thirty thousand?"

"Yes. I believe in taking care of my employees, so they take care of my business."

I stood, eased around the desk, and held my hand out to help her stand. "Let me show you out." As soon as her hand touched mine, an electric shock coursed through my body, amplifying the already bizarre attraction I was feeling toward her. This woman was so far out of the usual type I went for that it had me momentarily thrown off my game.

"Carlisle," I called out to my bar manager. "Miss Heart will be back tonight at eight for a trial run. If she does well, make it official."

"Yes, sir." He smiled from behind the granite countertop. "I'll see you later."

I watched as she walked toward the door. "Oh." She turned to face me. "What's the dress code?"

Carlisle answered before I could speak. "Black—pants and shirt or a dress. Though dresses will get you more tips." He actually fucking winked at her, eliciting a growl from me.

Madison blew out a breath and smiled. "Great, I'll see you tonight. Thanks again, Mr. Anastasi."

Her ass swayed as she hurried out the door, leaving me to stare at the wooden barrier. I had a million things to think about, but for some reason, the girl stood front and center in my thoughts.

"So you liked her?" Carlisle's voice cut through my haze.

"What?" I turned toward him.

"The girl, Madison. I was worried you'd hate her because, well…" He laughed. "She's not like the others we've hired in the past."

He was right about that. There was an innocence about her—something that I worried would come back to bite me in the ass. "Tonight will tell us if she can keep up or not. As much as she needs a job, I suspect she'll realize she's in over her head here." I shrugged, silently hoping I was wrong.

Turning on my heel, I headed in the direction of my private elevator. I needed to make a few calls, one of those to my father, to fill him in on the shit storm brewing. The last thing I needed was to worry myself with the new hire.

I pressed my thumb to the security pad, calling for the elevator. Regardless of how gorgeous she was, she was a temptation I didn't need, a beautiful distraction that could unravel the carefully controlled life I had built. As I reopened my eyes, the sounds of the club buzzed around me; a stark reminder of the life I led. I turned back inside, my resolve hardening. This trial run would tell me if she could handle the job. And I'd be able to see if I could handle being around her without losing control.

Because I was pretty certain this girl was going to be trouble.

MADISON

MY FEET WERE KILLING ME; the work was nothing like working for Gino's. The constant flow of people meant I hadn't sat down once. As I floated from patron to patron, I couldn't help but think about the rumors I had heard about the casino. Whispers floated around campus and in hushed conversations at coffee shops about the nightclub's dark affiliations. People said the mafia owned a chunk of businesses in Vegas, the club being one of them. The murmurs of shady dealings happening behind its glamorous facade and that working there paid a lot because—in their opinion—it could be dangerous.

These stories played on a loop in my head, creating a whirlwind of uncertainty. I had always prided myself on being cautious about making smart, calculated decisions. But now, desperation clawed at me from every angle. With no family to turn to and my savings dwindling to nothing, the luxury of choice had all but vanished. The stark reality was that I needed a job—any job—if I wanted to avoid sleeping on the streets.

"How's it going?" Carlisle, who would be my boss if I pulled this off, smiled at me from behind the bar. "You seem to be holding your own."

Glancing around the sultry atmosphere, I forced a smile. "It's definitely not Gino's."

I ran my hands down my front, straightening the clingy material. I was sure my measly black dress made me stand out among the other beautiful servers, who were all dressed like they belonged in Velvet Aces. Why Mr. Anastasi had given me a chance was beyond my comprehension. The women he employed were like something out of a movie. My idea of a safe job was a far cry from this. But I couldn't afford to be idealistic anymore, which is why I stood waiting for my drink order in a nightclub surrounded by beautiful people. But even as I tried to rationalize the decision, my thoughts were plagued by images of shadowy figures and illicit transactions. The logical part of me argued that these were just rumors, exaggerated tales designed to scare people.

After all, why would a prestigious nightclub risk its reputation by engaging in criminal activities?

Carlisle moved to the opposite end of the bar to wait on several ladies who'd gathered at the corner. Lost in thought, I startled when Julie, one of the other servers, bumped against my shoulder.

"Jesus, you scared the crap out of me." I cocked an eyebrow at the energetic woman standing beside me.

"You ready for a break? Carlisle said you've been busting your ass."

"A break?" I snorted as I scanned the packed casino. "I didn't figure you guys got those."

Julie rolled her eyes, a hint of amusement in her expression. "Mr. Anastasi isn't a dictator. He wants us to do our job, but not at the expense of killing ourselves. You'll learn. He takes really good care of his people, Madison."

I shifted uneasily. "I guess if you think it's okay. I don't want Mr. Anastasi to think I can't handle it here. I really need this job."

"Nah." Julie looped her arm through my elbow. "Let's go sit at the bar for a second and chat."

As she tugged me toward the bar, my eyes drifted to the man I'd run into earlier. His intense, hawkish gaze followed me, making me stop dead in my tracks. Julie noticed my sudden halt and turned her head, concern flickering in her eyes. "What's wrong?"

I nodded toward the man. "Who is that guy?" My voice did little to hide the nervousness I was feeling. Julie followed my gaze and laughed softly.

"That's Antonio Anastasi."

My heart skipped a beat. I turned to her, then glanced back at him. "He's an Anastasi?"

"Yep. There's a bunch of them. You'll probably meet Vincenzo and Catarina since they live here too, but the twins,

Celestina and Carmela, are hardly ever here—they're in Milan for school."

A wave of inadequacy washed over me. I was so out of my depth around these people. My mother died when I was a child, and my dad worked every day to make ends meet and put food on the table. He was my universe—until he wasn't. I'd thought we'd have a chance at a normal life after we lost my mom to violence.

I was wrong.

My dad's depression was too much, and it inevitably cost me him. At ten, I learned how harsh life was when I was thrust into foster care. The memory of my past pressed down on me, making me feel like an outsider in this world of prestige and power. How the hell was I going to pull off fitting in?

"Anyway," Julie's voice snapped me out of the dreadful place my mind was going. "He's the nice one—but don't tell anyone I said that."

"The others aren't nice?" I couldn't help but think about the rumors I had heard about the man in charge. "Should I be worried?"

Julie's blonde hair bounced with her laughter, and her carefree attitude eased some of my anxiety. "Unless you do something that they consider a betrayal, you don't have anything to worry about. Just do your job and keep your nose out of their business."

We slid up to the bar, and Carlisle greeted us with his typical charismatic smile. "Madison, what do you think so far?"

"I like it. So far, the clientele has been nice. By now, at my old job, I'd have already had my butt groped by a drunk watching the game."

"Well, we are a higher class of drunk here." He chuckled at his joke.

Julie's eyes widened, and I was about to ask her why when the heat of his voice washed over me. "If anyone so much as lays a hand on you, they won't like the consequences. I don't tolerate anyone touching what is mine—and that goes for my employees." Massimo stood casually behind me, his presence overwhelming.

I turned slowly to face him, my heart pounding in my chest. Massimo Anastasi was even more intimidating this close, and all the rumors I'd heard about him came flooding back. His eyes bored into mine, making me jump with surprise.

"Oh." I squeaked, realizing how near he was. "Um… Good evening, Mr. Anastasi—I was just taking a small break."

His eyes trailed my frame, his gaze almost making me feel as if he was undressing me with them. "It's fine; no need to explain, Miss Heart. My employees are entitled to a break. I'm not a monster."

Before I could respond, the guy leaving Mr. Anastasi's office, who I'd run into in the hallway earlier today, slid in beside me. "Hello, beautiful girl, we meet again." He pulled my hand to his mouth and brushed his lips against my knuckles, eliciting a growl from the man who held my fate in his hands. "Don't mind, my big brother. He's a grumpy bastard. How's your first night at the casino? Think you'll like working here?"

"I think so. But, ah…" I blushed, uncertain how I should respond. The man currently throwing pissed-off vibes had me terrified to say the wrong thing. "But it's not up to me."

Antonio smiled, and I could see how he was probably considered the nice one—hell, his smile nearly disarmed me, making me forget why I was standing there in the first place. "Well, you have my vote." He chuckled, making his brother growl again. "Shit, Massimo, you're scaring everyone."

"Good." He grumbled. "You can quit flirting with my employees—Julie and Madison—get back to work, or neither of you will work here any longer."

Antonio rolled his eyes as we watched a very angry Massimo turn on his heel and storm off.

"Crapsticks," I mumbled. "I really don't need the big boss ticked off at me. I need this job."

"Meh." Antonio waved his hand in the air. "Ignore him. He's a bit preoccupied with another issue. But, sadly, I need to head out. It was nice meeting you, Madison. I'm sure I'll see you around."

Antonio slipped off the stool he'd been occupying, and I couldn't help but search the club for his brother. The man scared me, not just because of the rumors surrounding him, but because the man himself was sexy as sin. At five foot nine, he had six inches on me, so I had to tilt my head anytime I wanted to look him in the eye. His hair was shaved short on the sides, but he had a mop of dark, unruly hair that always looked like he'd just woken up. His dark, nearly black eyes often looked like you were staring into pools of obsidian, giving him a menacing look.

Everything about the man screamed danger.

"Madison." Carlisle's voice carried over the music. "Looks like the boss is going to let me hire you. Congrats."

I blew out a breath, relief washing over me. "Thank god." I smiled at my new boss. "Guess I should go see who needs drinks."

Julie hurried off toward the second floor, leaving me alone with my thoughts. As I wandered the club, filling drinks, I couldn't help but feel like someone was watching me. Of course, no one ever was.

Leaving the bar, I hurried down the street. The night air was cool, a stark contrast to the warm, bustling atmosphere inside. Walking home at this hour was the only downside to my new job, but if it meant I could sleep easy and finish college—I'd take my chances. The city streets were quieter at this hour, shadows stretching long under the dim streetlights. I wrapped my arms around myself, both for warmth and a sense of security.

As I neared my apartment, I held my breath. It was the only thing I could afford, but it didn't mean I liked it. The complex was filled with drug addicts and women who paid their rent with their bodies. Stepping into the corridor, I paused when I saw my landlord leaning against my door.

Between his disgusting fingers was a glaring red paper. "Miss Heart." His voice made me want to puke. "Your rent is past due, *again*."

"I know. But I just got a new job and will have your money soon."

"Soon isn't enough." He pushed off the ratty door and stepped into my path. "I want your rent in the next week, unless you want to talk about another way to pay." He ran his grubby finger down my arm, making me shudder.

"Thanks, but I'll have your money." I stepped around him and managed to get my door open. Shoving inside the tiny apartment, I slammed the door behind me, and leaned against the cool wood. A wave of disgust and despair washed over me.

This wasn't the life I had envisioned for myself.

Working for Massimo Anastasi was going to be a challenge, but I was determined to prove myself. Even though I was pretty sure the scariest thing in town was the owner of my new job, this was my chance, and I wasn't going to let it slip away.

five

MASSIMO

I SAT in the large corner booth of the Velvet Lounge, and my brothers crowded around me as we discussed business. Antonio and Vincenzo sat on either side of me, their expressions mirroring my own—serious and focused.

"That the new waitress?" Vincenzo's gaze traveled the length of Madison's body. "She's hot—has she been upstairs yet?"

"No. And don't invite her," I barked, making his eyebrows shoot up in a sharp arch. The corners of his eyes crinkled slightly, as if trying to stifle a chuckle. His gaze held a mix of surprise and confusion, silently questioning my sudden outburst. "She doesn't fit in up there, and I'd rather not scare off my brand new employee with a flogger."

"Shit, Fratello, I just meant had she worked the second floor yet. Not had you taken her up there."

I was about to set his misguided assumption straight when Madison stopped at our table. "Um, sir, Mr. Anastasi. Gentlemen. Do you guys need anything?"

"Hey, doll." Antonio glanced over at me and smirked, knowing damn well he was pissing me off. "How has your first two weeks gone?"

"Err… I'm adjusting." She jerked a shoulder up. "It's hard work, but the money is worth it."

"Hard work is a part of life," I snapped, my words coming out harsher than I meant. "We can sleep when we're dead."

Madison visibly flinched at my words. Something about her past tickled in my memory, but I shrugged it off. My eyes narrowed, hardening into an icy glare that seemed to pierce through her. The chill in my gaze left no room for doubt about my feelings. "Get back to work and fetch us a bottle of Masseto."

She paled a little more before nodding. "Yes, sir."

Vincenzo smirked as she scurried off. "You don't have to be such an ass, Massimo. No need to treat her like a piece of shit."

"She needs to do her job without bitching. Now. Where were we?"

Across from us, Donny, my head enforcer, leaned forward, his bulk almost dwarfing the table between us. We were discussing a problem that had recently reared its ugly head— the missing guns.

"We've got a lead," Donny said, his voice a gravelly rumble. "One of our guys saw Juan Carlos's crew last night. They were loading crates onto a truck."

Antonio nodded, his jaw clenched. "We need to hit them back hard. Show them they can't mess with us."

I leaned back in my seat, running a hand through my hair. "Agreed. But we need to be smart about this. A direct attack could escalate things faster than we want. We need more information before I go to war with them."

Donny cleared his throat. "We need to figure out where they're keeping the guns. If we can get a location, we can plan our move."

Madison returned, this time with a tray of glasses and the two-thousand-dollar bottle of wine. She set them down with an infuriatingly calm expression. "Here you go."

"Good, now leave us alone." I knew I was being an asshole, but I needed to keep my walls up around her. She was a distraction I couldn't afford.

Antonio shook his head. "You're a real piece of work, you know that? Thank you, Madison. You'll have to excuse my brother… He's emotionally constipated."

I shrugged, feigning indifference. "Women are only good for one thing, and it's not interrupting meetings."

Madison stiffened, her face paling. She didn't say anything as she turned and walked away quickly. A pang of guilt hit me, but I shoved it aside. I couldn't afford to show weakness.

"Real classy," Vincenzo muttered. "You might want to apologize later."

"Noted," I said, though I had no intention of doing so. Apologizing would mean admitting she affected me, and I couldn't have that.

We continued our discussion, laying out plans for retribution. Donny suggested we bribe one of Juan Carlos's men for information, while Antonio advocated for a more direct approach: kidnapping one of their lieutenants and making him talk. Both plans had merit, but we needed to decide quickly before they created more problems for the family.

As the meeting wrapped up, my thoughts kept drifting back to Madison. Her presence was maddening and intriguing all at once, and I hated how she made me feel like I was seconds away from losing my carefully constructed control.

The club was starting to fill up for the night, and I could see Madison working the bar. Her movements called to me like a moth to a flame. She was good at her job, and I had to give her that because I hadn't expected her to last—she was far more innocent than the other employees. I watched as she laughed with a customer, her smile bright despite our earlier exchange. It twisted something inside me.

I couldn't afford to be distracted by Madison. Not now, not ever. My family came first, and right now, that meant dealing with Juan Carlos. Desperate to take my muddled thoughts off her, I headed toward my office. I hadn't made it far when Donny appeared, his face a mask of urgency.

"Boss," he glanced behind himself to ensure no one was around, which meant whatever he was about to say was not for prying ears. "Benito has Jose downstairs."

"What? How?"

"It looks like Jose pissed off some of his fellow foot soldiers. It didn't take long for one of them to turn on him when they heard you were looking for him. In fact, Miguel Angel is waiting at the bar to see you. He's the one who brought him to us."

Sitting at the bar was a Hispanic male. He was dressed in a business suit and had an air of class about himself, not someone who belonged to one of the most ruthless Mexican gangs on the street.

"Miguel." I approached him with my hand extended. "I understand you've brought me a gift."

"Mr. Anastasi." He shook my hand. "Is there somewhere we can speak…privately?"

I led him back to my office, the weight of curiosity and caution settling on my shoulders. Donny closed the door, cutting us off from any prying ears. The tension in the room was palpable as we stared one another down.

"Why did you bring Jose to me? You two work for the same man."

"Sir, Juan Carlos has taken a once-admired organization and turned it into nothing but a group of thugs. I have stood by and watched the spiral as he turned the Sureños into a shit show. A few of us disagreed with his tactics. To run a successful operation, you have to work together—but Juan didn't see it that way."

Miguel's voice held a blend of frustration and determination. I could see the fire in his eyes, the same fire that fueled my own ambitions. There was more to this meeting than a simple handover.

"I've been thinking," Miguel continued, leaning forward, his voice dropping to a conspiratorial whisper. "Juan Carlos is a cancer to our operations. He's reckless and his decisions are leading us all to ruin. We need someone with vision, someone who can bring order back to the Sureños. That someone is me."

I raised an eyebrow. "And why are you telling me this? Why bring me, Jose?"

"Because, Mr. Anastasi, I need your help to remove Juan Carlos from power. With your family's support, I can take over and lead the Sureños back to the organization it once was. This union would include a profitable alliance with the Anastasi family. We can build something greater together, something powerful. But first, Juan Carlos must go."

The room fell silent as I processed his words. This was a bold move, a risky proposition, but the potential benefits were undeniable. Under the right leadership, an alliance with the Sureños would considerably strengthen our position in Vegas.

"And what assurance do I have you'll keep your word once Juan Carlos is out of the picture?" I asked, my tone edged with skepticism. "Because you know what would happen if you betrayed us."

Miguel leaned back, his expression unflinching. "I'm a man of my word, Mr. Anastasi. You help me take down Juan Carlos, and I promise you fidelity. Together, we can bring order back to our streets and ensure our mutual success."

"I need to speak with my father. I'm sure you understand."

Miguel nodded as he pushed to his feet and moved to leave. "I wouldn't expect anything less, Mr. Anastasi." He pulled open the door slightly and paused. "In the meantime, consider Jose a token of my loyalty. Any man who steals from the inside deserves to die a painful death."

A gasp had all three of us turning toward the hallway. Madison stood just outside my door, her eyes widening as she visibly paled, clearly indicating she'd heard what Miguel said.

Staring at her, I had to force myself to breathe. My chest tightened, and I felt the heat rising from my neck to my face. "Can I help you?" It came out more like a growl, laced with the frustration of being thrown off my game.

"I uh…" Her gaze flicked nervously between the men in the room, "Sorry, Carlisle said to come get you—your sister is at the bar and um… She's had a little too much to drink."

Miguel's eyes trailed over her body in a lecherous way, lingering on her curves. "Excuse me, pretty girl." He turned back to look at me, his smile sharp and predatory. "Perhaps I should hang out here more often."

The growl in my throat deepened. "My employees are off limits to you—otherwise, this deal is off before it begins."

His gaze narrowed slightly, calculating, before he forced it to relax. "Ah… I see. Well, I can't blame you; she is beautiful." He returned his gaze to Madison, his smile still wolfish. "Don't let the big bad wolf eat you alive."

With that, he edged around a stunned Madison and left. The room felt a bit lighter without his oppressive presence, but the tension still clung to the air.

Donny growled softly, his eyes darkening. "I'll deal with Catarina."

I nodded, knowing there was something more between my enforcer and my sister, but I didn't press the issue. It wasn't the time or place, and I trusted Donny to handle whatever situation had arisen. He hurried out of the office, leaving Madison alone with me. I leaned back in my chair, watching her with a mixture of annoyance and something I didn't want to admit.

"You need to watch yourself, Madison," I said, my voice low and dangerous. "Interrupting my meetings won't end the way you want it to."

Her eyes widened, filling with unshed tears, but she stood her ground, her voice barely a whisper. "I-I'm sorry, Mr. Anastasi. I didn't mean to interrupt. I was just doing what Carlisle asked me to do."

I'd be talking to Carlisle next. "You're lucky to have a job at the club," I continued, letting my gaze rake over her with deliberate intensity. "You're a far cry from the women I usually hire." I let the insinuation hang in the air.

She nodded, her lips trembling, tears threatening to spill over. "I understand, sir," she whispered, her voice cracking as she held my gaze. Her innocence was so out of place in my world. She stood out like sunshine among the dark clouds, something I found both intriguing and confusing.

The vulnerability in her eyes made something twist inside me, but I couldn't afford to soften. She nodded again, more to herself this time, and hurried out of my office. The door slammed behind her, and I slammed my fists onto my desk, frustrated at how fucked up she made me feel.

She was becoming more of a complication I didn't need yet couldn't seem to ignore.

MADISON

FOR THREE WEEKS, I'd been working for Massimo Anastasi, and for three weeks, I'd nearly quit every day. Not because I couldn't handle the work. No, I'd considered walking out the door because that man is a terrifying, overbearing, butthole.

Climbing the steps up to my sad apartment, I reminded myself why I couldn't let his rude personality run me off—even if he had reminded me time after time that I didn't fit in. I'd finally got my rent current and felt good until I got to the top of the steps and saw what was waiting for me.

My door had been busted in, leaving it hanging on one hinge. Racing inside, my breath left my lungs when I saw the damage to what little belongings I had. My couch had been cut up, leaving foam and stuffing strewn all over the floor. The dresser was tipped on its side, and the drawers and what little clothing I had were scattered across the apartment.

Whoever had broken in, messed up the door something awful. I tried to wedge it back over the opening, but quickly realized there was no way to fix it. I leaned it against the wall to get my bearings and steady my breathing. Once I called 9-1-1 and managed to get myself slightly composed, I headed over to my building manager's apartment. I didn't really talk to the other people in my building because they were usually drunk or high, but I needed him to come to deal with the broken door because the thought of leaving it open left me on the verge of a panic attack.

Knocking on the door across the hall from me, I waited. I could hear someone walking toward the front of the apartment. The door opened in a whoosh.

"What the fuck do you want?" The man was only wearing a pair of basketball shorts and reeked of weed.

"Someone broke into my apartment." I swiped at the tears gathering in my eyes. "The door is messed up." I stepped back when his eyes roamed my body. "Seriously, Kyle. I don't have time for this.." My voice cracked with emotion. "My stuff is destroyed, and I have to be at work. I can't leave it like this, and I know you want your rent on time, but I have to leave."

"Did you call the cops?"

I held my pre-paid phone up and waved it in the air. "Of course I did, you knobhead—my apartment was broken into, but the door–" I waved at the cracked frame, "Won't shut."

Kyle glanced at my place and then back at me, a smirk curling on his lips. "You think anyone's gonna steal your thrift store furniture and worn-out clothes? Please. No one's interested in your stuff, Madison."

My blood boiled at his dismissive tone, but I forced myself to stay calm. "It's not about what's in my apartment, Kyle. It's about my safety. I need the door fixed."

He shrugged, the smirk never leaving his face. "I'll get to it when I get to it. Maybe later today. Or tomorrow. We'll see."

"That's unacceptable," I snapped. "I'm telling the cops when they get here that you're refusing to do anything. As my *land-lord,* you have a responsibility to me, *your* tenant."

Kyle rolled his eyes. "Go ahead." The wood hit me in the nose as he slammed it closed.

Ignoring his infuriating lack of concern, I waited in the hall for the police. Within fifteen minutes, two officers arrived. One, a stocky man with a receding hairline, took my statement while the other, a younger woman with kind eyes, inspected the door.

"So, nothing was taken?" the older officer asked, his tone almost bored.

"Nothing I can see," I confirmed. "But the door won't shut properly, and it makes me feel unsafe."

The younger officer nodded sympathetically. "We understand your concern, ma'am. Unfortunately, since there wasn't any theft, it's unlikely we'll find much. We can file a report, but…"

"But it won't help," I finished for her, feeling the weight of the situation settle over me.

"Right," she admitted. "We recommend getting the door fixed as soon as possible and maybe consider upgrading your locks."

After the police left, I felt even more frustrated and helpless. Kyle was back in his apartment, probably laughing at my expense. I couldn't leave my place unsecured, so I pulled out my phone and called Carlisle, my boss. His steady voice on the other end brought a rush of relief.

"Hey, Madison. What's up?" he answered cheerfully.

"Carlisle, Sorry to call this short notice, but I'm going to be late for work. Something came up," I said, trying to keep my voice steady. I didn't want to give away too much over the phone.

"Everything okay?" he asked, concern creeping into his voice.

"Yeah, just…apartment stuff. I'll explain later. I just wanted to give you a heads-up." There was no telling when Kyle would actually fix the door.

"All right," he drawled. "Take care of what you need to. We'll manage here."

"Thanks. I'll be in as soon as I can." I hung up, taking a deep breath to steady myself.

Realizing that waiting for Kyle was pointless, I decided to change my clothes and go to work anyway. Losing pay wasn't going to help matters at all. After changing out of the clothes I'd worn to my morning class, I tugged the flimsy door shut and secured my messenger bag across my chest. I wasn't about to leave my laptop inside—it was way too important to me and held my entire life and everything I was working for in it. I was lucky it hadn't been taken.

I held the bag against my chest, hurried down the stairs, and headed to work. I was used to the walk, but tonight, it felt different. My home had been violated, leaving me feeling unprotected. My thoughts drifted back to a time I'd worked hard to overcome—lord knew I would never forget about it.

I'd become hardened to life at an early age. My mother died when I was a child during a home invasion. I watched her murder happen from a bedroom closet where she'd hidden me. She left to call for help, but they caught her before she had a chance and shot her in the head. My dad wasn't home when it happened, thank God, because I would have been orphaned. Little did I know, only a year later, it would happen anyway.

He worked every day to make ends meet and put food on the table. My dad was my universe—until he wasn't. He began drinking to cope with the stress of raising a daughter on his own and losing the love of his life so violently. With counseling, I'd managed to be a normal kid. Well, as much as I could be after witnessing her death. I'd thought we'd have a chance at a normal life again.

I was *wrong*.

The lights of the casino drew me out of my memory. Shaking off the dark thoughts, I forced a smile as I stepped up to the entrance. Oscar, the bouncer, though I suspected he was more than that, stood at the door. His body resembled a linebacker, solid and, well…scary as frick. His arms were as big around as my thighs, and that was saying something because I was a thick girl. But Oscar was nothing more than a giant teddy bear.

"Miss Heart." He smiled. "Thought you were gonna be later than this?"

Shrugging my shoulders, I said, "Turns out there was no point in fixing the issue, so here I am." I patted his arm. "Looks busy."

Oscar grunted. "There's a private party tonight. Usually means more drama, but it's good money for the club."

"All right, I'll head in and get ready. See ya later, Oscar."

Carlisle looked up from behind the bar when he spotted me. His expression was a mix of curiosity and concern. "Hey, Maddie, everything good?"

I nodded and plastered a smile on my face. I didn't want anyone to feel sorry for the poor girl, so I had no intention of telling him why I was late. "Yeah, I managed to sort it out. Can I put this behind the bar? I, uh…might do some home-work if I get a break." The lie rolled off my tongue as I glanced around the packed-out lounge. "Though from the looks of it, might not happen."

He waved off my apology. "Meh—you know you can take a break later. Here," he said, holding out his hand. I'll stash it back here. If you need it later, let me know."

"Thanks, Carlisle," I said, appreciating his understanding. "Guess I should get to work; this crowd is insane."

As the night wound down, I found myself leaning against the bar. "Tonight was crazy. I'm sorry I was late."

Carlisle smiled. "It wasn't a problem."

"It was a problem." The growl behind me made me stiffen. "And you being late put everyone in a bind." *His* voice washed over me, and I slowly turned to face the man who I wanted to avoid. "If you aren't going to take this job seriously, maybe you shouldn't be here."

"I had an issue—" He held his hand up, cutting off my words.

"I don't give a fuck, Miss Heart. I expect my employees to show up...on *time*." He turned on his heel. "Carlisle," he barked his name. "See me in my office."

Carlisle gave me a reassuring smile. "It's all good. See you tomorrow, Maddie." He turned and headed toward the office.

"Don't worry about him." Julie's sudden presence made me jump. "He's pissed off about something else."

"Well," I turned to her, "It's not like I asked for my apartment to be broken into." Julie gasped, but I shrugged her reaction off. "It's no big deal. I didn't have anything they wanted."

"Doesn't matter. You should tell him about it, Madison. If anything, it'd make him feel like an asshole for his reaction."

I snorted. "I doubt that, Julie. The man is perpetually grumpy. I don't know anything that would make him feel something other than—I don't know, bitterness."

Julie smirked, her eyes glittering with something that looked like trouble. "I can't wait until someone knocks that man down off his high horse."

"It's going to take a miracle for that to happen." I reached over the bar and grabbed my bag. "And I don't believe in those."

seven

MASSIMO

I PACED BACK and forth inside my office as Carlisle leaned against the wall. "How many times has she been late?"

Carlisle straightened. "This was the first time, sir, since she started working here."

"If it happens again, fire her."

Carlisle bit down on his lip before speaking. "All due respect, sir, don't you think that's a bit harsh? Maddie has been an asset to the staff, and it was the first time. I'm certain whatever caused her to be a half hour late was something major."

I was about to rip him a new asshole when Julie's voice cut through the tension.

"It was. Her apartment was broken into today."

"What?" Carlisle's eyes widened. "She didn't say anything."

"Why would she?" Julie swallowed, her nerves obvious. "That girl is the most private person I've ever met. Did you know she walks to work every day? She doesn't own a car. And the cell she carries is a pre-paid one. I'm pretty sure she was barely surviving before this job—and firing her over being thirty minutes late is shitty even for you… Mr. Anastasi, sir."

Julie hardened her spine; I was sure she was waiting for me to lash out. But my mind was stuck on her words. *Madison walked to work.* I knew from her background she didn't live in the nicest area. And hearing her apartment had been broken into triggered something vicious inside me.

I slid my cell phone from my pocket and made a quick call. "Freddy, pull my car around." I disconnected and made the next call to Donny. "Meet me out front. We're going for a ride."

Julie stepped back. "Um…are you going to fire me?"

"No." I pushed around her, and both she and Carlisle closed on my heel. "But if you ever keep something important about one of my employees from me or speak to me that way again, you won't be so lucky."

"Yes, sir." She whispered her response so my point was clear.

As soon as I stepped outside, Donny was leaning against my awaiting car. "What's up?"

"We're going to Miss Heart's place. I've just been informed she had a break-in and didn't bother to tell anyone."

"Oh?" He cocked his head in confusion. "And we're going there, why?"

"Don't question me, Donny, just get in the fucking car."

We had almost made it to her complex when I spotted her. Donny said, "What the fuck? Is that her walking—*here*?" Donny was a brutal bastard like me, but when it came to women, he believed it was a man's job to protect her.

"Yep. Freddy, stop the car." The car barely stopped before I pushed open my door. "Madison," I called out, her body jumping at the sound of her name. Even from my distance, I could see she had been crying, her eyes red and swollen.

"Mr. Anastasi?" She glanced at me, then to Donny, who'd also slipped out of the car. "Did I forget to do something?"

I stepped forward, closing the distance between us. "Get in the car, Miss Heart."

"What?" She moved out of my reach.

Impatience washed over me, and I snapped my hand out and wrapped it around her arms. "Don't make me ask twice. Get. In. The. Car."

"Miss Heart." Donny had moved around the car to stand beside her. "We're here to help you, please." He sighed. "Get in the car before the ogre tosses you inside."

She blinked, her gaze flicking between the two of us. "I don't understand what's happening right now." She pulled free of my grasp and slipped into the back seat.

Donny smirked at me. "Maybe cool off the caveman act. You're scaring the shit out of her." If Donny had been anyone else, I probably would have put a bullet between his eyes, but he wasn't just my most trusted enforcer; he was my best friend. Growing up together had forged a close bond, giving him liberties others could not take when speaking to me.

"Fuck off." I scooted in beside her and slammed the door. Donny climbed in the front and shook his head. "Miss Heart." I turned to her, "It was brought to my attention that you were late due to a break-in at your apartment. Why didn't you tell me?"

She snorted, "Why? Would you have threatened my employment differently? I'm sorry." She looked up at me, embarrassment marring her beautiful face. "You don't need to deal with my mess."

As soon as we stopped in front of her building, I watched as she opened the door and climbed out.

"I wouldn't have come out here if I was concerned about dealing with your bullshit. Tell me what happened." I slipped out behind her and angled myself close to her body. I brushed my hand down her back.

"When I got home, my door was smashed in. Someone had broken in." Tears streamed down her face. "Luckily, they didn't get this." She tapped the bag she cradled against her side.

Grabbing her arms, I pulled her body against mine, and rage unlike anything I'd ever felt coursed through my veins. "You should have told me."

She tensed at my harsh tone and stammered her words. "Why? You're my boss, and It's not important. They only busted through the door and destroyed my stuff."

"It matters." I held her gaze. "And you can call me Massimo," I smirked at her stunned expression. "Did you call the police or your landlord?" I looked down at the woman cradled against me and realized the distance I was determined to keep from her was slowly fading.

"Yes, and neither were helpful." I followed her up the rickety stairs. I had to stifle the swear words when I saw her door. She'd pulled it closed when she left, but it was crooked and might as well have been left open.

"Wait here, please." I motioned to Donny to go in before us. "Donny is just going to check it out before we go in."

"I was here earlier." She grunted her displeasure at my insistence on controlling the situation. "I'm sure it's fine."

"That may be true, but amuse me."

Donny stepped out of her apartment. "It's a disaster. But otherwise, all clear, boss."

I scanned the room, disgust lacing my expression. Her apartment was one step above a hovel. "Where's your bed?"

Madison's shoulders dropped. "I sleep on the couch. We don't all live in the lap of luxury."

"You can't stay here." I turned to Donny. "Call Antonio. Have him send someone here in the morning to fix the mess."

"Yes, sir." Donny walked out, leaving me alone with her.

"That's unnecessary." Madison's voice was meek. "I'm sure my landlord is going to take care of it, even if he slammed his door in my face and acted like it's no big deal. Besides, I can always stay at a hotel tonight."

"No." I took a steadying breath. I was going to kill the motherfucker. Madison followed me into the hallway. I pointed to the door and growled. "Is that the landlord's place?

"Yes, but," she grabbed my arm, "what are you doing?" I looked where her dainty fingers latched onto my arm, surprised that she was touching me. My expression must have startled her because she jerked away, putting space between us.

I stormed over to the prick's door and slammed my fist against the wood. "Come on, this is stupid. Why do you need to talk to him?" Madison yanked on my sleeve, trying to stop me.

The guy opened the door. "What the fuck do you want?"

I reached through the open door and grabbed him by the throat. "Did she—" I pointed to a very stunned Madison standing behind me— "ask you for your help earlier?"

"What?" He clawed at my fingers wrapped around his skinny neck, trying to peel them away. Squeezing harder, noting he was on the verge of losing consciousness, I didn't stop. "I don't know." He squeaked out his response as his nails dug into my arm.

Using my free hand, I grabbed his finger off me and bent it, the sickening sound of the bone snapping between us. "Look at her." He turned his eyes toward her. "Did. She. Ask. For. Help?"

When he didn't answer, I twisted another finger, making Madison gasp. "Stop… Massimo, please."

The sound of my name on her lips had me glance in her direction. The fear written all over her face nearly gutted me. I stepped back, making room for Donny, who smacked him across the face ."Do you know who he is?"

"Yes." He garbled as his eyes sought out Madison.

"Don't fucking look at her." I grabbed him again and slammed his body against the wall. His scream of pain echoed through the hallway as I jabbed my elbow into his chest. "Good. Then you know you fucked up when you turned her away. Donny," I let my fist fly. The crunching sound of his nose was satisfying as I watched the fucker drop to the floor, cradling his face. "Clean up this trash and meet us back at the club."

"Yes, sir." Donny stepped forward, snatched the sorry excuse of a man off the ground, and dragged him into his apartment. I knew what Donny was capable of, so leaving him in the very demented hands of my best friend was enough for me.

"Let's go." I turned to Madison. "You're not staying here."

"I'm not going anywhere with you." She backed up, but I was quicker and grabbed her.

"Don't make me carry you out of here."

"You wouldn't dare." Her eyes held shock when I leaned down and slung her body over my shoulder.

"Don't ever dare me, Madison," I growled.

This woman had burrowed her way under my skin, and despite my best efforts to stay away, I'd failed. I felt her fists pound against my back, her protests muffled by the blood rushing in my ears. Her scent, a mix of vanilla and fear, filled my senses, making me more determined to protect her.

As we reached the street, I set her down, her eyes blazing with anger. "You can't just do that! You can't just manhandle me like some possession!"

I stepped closer, my voice dropping to a whisper. "I will do whatever it takes to keep you safe, Madison. Even if it means crossing every line."

Her defiance wavered, her eyes searching mine for some sign of softness, some hint of the man I was beneath the ruthlessness. "I don't need your protection," she whispered, but her voice trembled.

"Yes, you do." I brushed a strand of hair from her face, my touch lingering. "And I'm not going to let you out of my sight until I know you're safe."

As we walked to the car, I couldn't help but feel a strange sense of peace. Madison was more than just an employee. She was becoming something I craved, like a drug, and I wasn't about to let anything happen to her. Letting myself want her was wrong, but I wasn't about to fight it anymore—dangerous attraction or not, she was going to be mine.

I crossed a line, and there was no going back. She was going to be mine, and nothing was going to happen to this woman.

Not while I was breathing.

MADISON

WHAT IN THE heck was happening?

I'd just watched my boss break several fingers on my land-lord's hand before laying him out on the floor. Not to mention, I was pretty sure Donny was doing far worse to him. Finally mustering my courage, I spoke.

"Where are we going?"

"To my apartment." Massimo pointed to the top floor of the Velvet Ace as the car slowed to a stop.

"I told you I could go to a hotel."

"Madison, please don't make me carry you inside. You're not staying at a hotel, and I can't let you out of my sight right now."

I stared at him, wanting to scream. Everything about the situation was messed up. My boss, who I'd thought up until this moment hated my guts, had come to my rescue. I didn't deserve his help or hospitality, but nothing about this situation made sense. Like a mindless dummy, I got out of the car and followed him inside. The club was empty. The darkness had me stepping closer to his tall frame as we waited by the elevator.

"Come on." His deep voice drew me from the thoughts swirling in my head as he motioned for me to climb inside the metal box. "This one takes you to my apartment upstairs. Only I have access, so you'll be safe here."

His apartment was five times the size of mine. It was an open floor plan with a stylish chrome kitchen. The living space was furnished with sleek black furniture–fitting for a man who I assumed had a black heart, at least until tonight. A door led off to what I assumed was the bathroom. Immediately, my eyes noted the large bed toward the back of the apartment—*one* bed.

There's only one bed." I met his watchful eyes, my heart pounding in my chest.

A knowing smirk touched his lips as he spoke. "I know." Massimo walked into the kitchen and grabbed some whiskey from a cabinet. "You want one?"

I followed him into the kitchen, my mind racing. "Massimo, where am I going to sleep?"

He smiled, pouring the smooth liquid into two glasses. "The bed." He lifted the drink to his lips, his eyes never straying from me.

I swallowed, my nerves flickering with worry. "And you?"

He set the glass down on the counter with a deliberate slowness that only heightened my anxiety. "The bed."

"What? No…" I twisted my hands, and I was on the verge of throwing up. How had my night taken such a weird turn? My pulse quickened, and I could feel the heat rising to my cheeks.

Sensing my unease, I watched as the corner of his mouth quirked up in a half-smile. "I'll take the couch."

I glanced toward the massive leather monstrosity taking up a lot of space. "That's your bed. I can sleep on the couch. It's nicer than mine, anyway. It'll be fine."

Massimo pushed the tumbler away from himself and stepped into my space, his presence both comforting and intimidating. He placed a hand on my hip, tugging my body closer. My breath hitched as his other hand pressed beneath my chin, forcing me to look into his intense gaze.

"You're sleeping in my bed. That's not up for debate. My mother raised me to be a gentleman. Now…" He dropped his hand from my face, the warmth of his touch lingering. "Have you eaten?"

The switch in conversation left me momentarily stunned. My stomach growled in response, betraying my nerves. "No, I haven't," I admitted, my voice barely above a whisper.

"Let's fix that, then," he said, a genuine smile breaking through his smirk as he began pulling things out of his cabinets.

"I'm not staying here," I said, my voice firmer than I felt. My hands gripped the strap of my bag, ready to make my escape.

Massimo didn't look up from where he was chopping vegetables with the precision of a surgeon. "You are," he replied calmly, his deep voice steady, as if we were simply discussing the weather.

"Massimo, I appreciate the gesture, but I should be at a hotel," I insisted, trying to inject some steel into my wavering resolve. "I don't want to intrude."

Standing in Massimo's kitchen, I felt like an interloper in a place where I didn't belong. The sleek countertops, the minimalist decor, the scent of something mouth-wateringly delicious simmering on the stove—it all screamed Massimo. This was his domain, and I was a reluctant guest.

He finally looked up, his dark eyes locking onto mine with an intensity that made my breath catch. "You're not intruding, Madison. You're staying here. End of discussion."

I took a step back; the cool tile under my feet did nothing to calm my racing thoughts. "You can't just decide that for me," I argued, but it sounded weak, even to my own ears.

He set the knife down and walked around the island, closing the distance between us. "I can, and I have," he said, his tone softer but no less resolute. "It's late, you're exhausted, and this city can be… unpredictable at night. You're safer here."

"Safer?" I repeated, incredulous. "Massimo, it's not about safety. It's about boundaries. You're my boss."

"I could fire you." He sighed, running a hand through his hair in a rare display of frustration. "Madison, for once, can you just trust me? I'm not trying to cross any lines. I just want you to be comfortable and safe."

I glanced around the kitchen, my eyes landing on a photo of Massimo with an older woman who must've been his mother, both of them smiling warmly. It was a glimpse into a life I found unexpected, a side of him surprisingly softer. It made me feel even more out of place.

"But this is your home," I whispered, the fight draining out of me. "It feels wrong."

He ignored my statement, his focus on the task of making food. It's weird seeing this powerful man making pasta while wearing a suit—he seemed so out of place right now. "How do you like your pasta? Al dente or softer?"

I opened my mouth to protest again, but the look in his eyes stopped me. There was something almost pleading in his gaze, a vulnerability I didn't expect. Maybe he wasn't being the overbearing boss. Maybe he genuinely cared.

"Al dente," I murmured, giving in just a little and setting my bag on the ground beside the stool.

"Good choice." His tone was harsher than I expected, seeing as I had given in to his ridiculous demands.

"Why are you so mad? I don't understand what's happening right now." I rubbed my face, the events of the day finally wearing on me. "If me being here is an issue you can just take me to a hotel—like I've been asking you."

His body tensed. "Don't ask me again, Madison." He glanced up from the stove. "You won't like it if you keep pushing me on this."

He plated the food and slid it across the table to me. "Here, eat, and then you can take a shower."

I picked up a fork, my eyes watching Massimo as he began to strip off his jacket. My gaze narrowed on the leather strap securing the gun beneath his arm. The utensil clattered against the plate. Deep down, I knew the stories were true about my boss—heck, I'd just witnessed him brutalize my landlord for not helping me, but seeing the gun was different.

It meant all the rumors I'd been hearing were probably true.

I excused myself, barely keeping my voice steady, and stood up. The stool scraped against the floor with a harsh, grating sound, its legs dragging reluctantly over the surface. The noise echoed sharply through the room, punctuating the otherwise quiet atmosphere. "I can't be here."

My heart pounded as I walked away, feeling Massimo's eyes bore into my back. I pushed open the door to the bathroom and shut myself inside. I leaned against the sink, gripping the porcelain edge until my knuckles turned white. The tears came unbidden, hot and angry. The image of my mother's lifeless body—the horror frozen on her face—haunted my dreams even now. I had vowed never to be a part of that world, to distance myself from the violence that had stolen her from me.

The bathroom door creaked open, and I hastily wiped my eyes, straightening up. Massimo stood in the doorway, his expression unreadable. For a moment, neither of us spoke. The silence stretched between us, heavy with unspoken words. He'd discarded the weapon, and his sleeves were rolled up, exposing the muscular forearms beneath.

"Madison," he began, his palms braced against the opening of the bathroom.

I shook my head, the panic rising. "I–please, I can't be here, Massimo."

His eyes softened as he spoke, "You can't leave, Madison, not until I know you're safe. Take a shower—we'll talk when you're done. But I promise… I won't hurt you."

I hesitated, the conflict raging inside me. The rational part of me screamed to leave, to walk away and never look back. But the part of me that was weirdly coming to care for him, the part that saw glimpses of the man beneath the cold exterior, held me back.

Too exhausted to argue anymore, I simply nodded. He backed out, pulling the door closed as he did. I turned on the shower, and the sound of the water was a brief respite from the chaos in my mind.

I took a deep breath, bracing myself for whatever came next. Because despite everything, a part of me still wanted to believe in him. And maybe, just maybe, that part was right.

nine

MASSIMO

FORCING MYSELF, I left her alone and collapsed onto the couch. Hearing the water running, knowing she was getting undressed on the other side of the door, left me uncomfortable. My dick was growing hard with visions of her smooth, naked skin beneath the water.

Why had I suggested she come here? It was going to be nearly impossible to keep my hands off her. The rattling of my phone on the table caused me to jerk upright.

"What?"

Donny grunted into the phone. "Sorry, boss, but we got a problem. One of the other drivers is dead."

"Where?" I leaned forward and pressed my elbows to my knees.

"Behind The Sapphire Dagger in the alleyway."

"Fuck." I stood and moved to the massive window. It was the

only set of windows in the space, but they took up the entire wall. "Think its related to the other matter?"

"Yeah. It looks professional, even though they tried to make it look otherwise."

I blew out a frustrated breath. "Any leads on the merchandise?"

"Nope. Whoever did this is trying to clean up some loose ends."

Blowing out a frustrated breath, I ran my fingers through my hair. "Go through the driver's house. See if there's anything there that will help us connect him to the missing cargo."

I turned, finding Madison standing in the doorway with nothing but a towel wrapped around her body. Her legs disappeared beneath the white cotton fabric she was clutching in her fingers, giving me enough view of her perfect skin underneath.

"I need to take care of some things. Let me know what you find." I hung up and slipped my phone in my pocket. "Everything all right?"

"I don't have anything to wear."

"Shit." I pushed inside the bathroom and into my walk-in closet. Jerking down one of my dress shirts, I thrusted it at her. "Here."

She tried to grab it with one hand, but it slipped from her grasp and hit the floor. Bending down, I grabbed it—which put me at eye level with the pussy hidden beneath the fabric. I closed my eyes and willed myself to stop staring at her. We were so close I could've just lifted the towel and buried my face between her legs. Instead, I forced myself to stand, holding the shirt tightly in my grasp.

"Why are you doing this for me? You barely know me."

"I don't know," I whispered, running my thumb over her plump lip.

Madison took a deep breath as she held my gaze. I could see the confusion in her eyes—confusion I was sure mirrored back.

"Get dressed before I change my mind about being a gentleman."

As I stepped around her, she finally spoke. "I reacted poorly because of the gun," she admitted softly. "I've had a rough past with them, and they just…trigger me."

I paused, turning back to her. "I know about your past," I said gently. "But I promise you, I'm one of the good guys. You aren't in danger with me."

I could see the exhaustion etched on her face, the way her shoulders slumped, and the slight tremor in her hands. "Come on," I said, taking her hand and leading her to the bed. "You need to get some sleep. It's well past midnight, and I can see how tired you are."

She hesitated for a moment before allowing me to guide her. "Under the covers," I ordered softly. "Sleep. I'm going to change."

I turned around and forced my feet to carry me into the bathroom and shut the door. This woman was slowly tearing apart my perfectly controlled atmosphere. Stripping out of my clothes, I ignored the way my cock hardened from thoughts of Madison laid out on my bed. Giving my dick a small tug, I groaned before tugging on a pair of shorts. Now wasn't the time to indulge in fantasies about the woman just beyond my bathroom door.

The sound of the door made Madison's eyes snap open. I froze in the entryway as her eyes scanned my body. I wasn't dumb, I knew how I looked, and the pair of basketball shorts left little to the imagination. Not to mention my dick was still semi-hard, which meant it was clearly outlined beneath the clingy fabric. And the way her eyes were staring at it, there was no way I could hide my reaction to her.

"Go to bed, Madison," I growled, stomping my way to the couch, frustration rippling through me like an electric current. Her sigh filled the room, a sound heavy with regret.

Her sigh filled the room. "I feel bad. Seriously, that couch looks way more comfortable than the one I sleep on in my apartment. You should be in your bed, not me."

I turned sharply, my feet driving into the floor with each step. Her eyes widened as I approached, and I could see the flicker of surprise when I stopped inches away, leaning down and trapping her between my arms on the bed.

"You will take my bed. Do you understand me?" My voice was a low growl, leaving no room for argument.

"Yes." Her words squeaked out, almost inaudible.

"Good." I kept her caged in, my eyes roaming over her body.

Massimo," she breathed, her voice barely a whisper charged with tension.

To someone walking in on us, it would look like we were in an intimate position.

"What are you doing to me?" My voice was husky, laced with an intensity I couldn't control as I stared down at her. I could see the internal battle raging behind her eyes, mirroring my own turmoil. "Get some rest. We'll talk about what to do about your place tomorrow."

Turning my back to her, I snatched the spare comforter off the end of the bed and walked to the couch. The fabric rustled softly as I settled in, but sleep remained elusive. I could hear her moving around in the bed, making it impossible for me to close my eyes.

"Massimo?" she whispered into the dark, her voice filled with uncertainty.

The couch groaned with my movement. "Something wrong?" I grunted, trying to keep my irritation in check.

"I can't sleep."

"Do you need another blanket?"

"No... I..." She sighed into the room, a sound filled with vulnerability. "This place is foreign to me. Do you think you could come lay beside me?"

"You want me to get into bed with you?" I asked, disbelief coloring my words.

"I know it's silly because we don't know each other, but I'm scared to close my eyes."

The couch creaked as I stood, my resolve melting away. My feet made a slight thumping sound as I padded across the room. The bed dipped on the opposite side as I climbed in beside her, the mattress enveloping us in its warmth.

"Go to sleep." I murmured, my voice softer now, almost gentle.

"Thank you, Massimo…for everything." Her words hung in the air between us, a fragile bridge connecting two souls that couldn't be any more different.

I pinched my eyes closed and willed sleep to tug me under. I couldn't believe I was lying in bed beside Madison. I'd never had a woman I wasn't fucking in bed before, and never one in my personal space. The silence told me she'd finally gone to sleep. Closing my eyes, I prayed for my erection to go away so I could get some sleep as well. Taking a couple of deep breaths and letting them out, I clenched my hands. As much as I wanted to touch her, I needed to give her time. Madison was the most innocent woman I'd ever been around and she needed to be ready for what I offered, and right now, she was too vulnerable.

Movement in the bed caught me off guard as an arm draped across my stomach. Opening my eyes, I realized Madison had rolled over in her sleep, snuggling against my body. I debated whether to wake her, finally deciding to leave it alone. It wasn't like I was hurting from the current position I was in… well, not really.

If she moved her arm any lower, she would notice the hard-on I was sporting. She shifted again, pressing her head into the crook of my shoulder as she snuggled her body next to mine. Giving up on keeping my hands to myself, I wrapped my arm around her and tugged her against me. She wiggled and blew out a breath of warm air against my skin, the sensation creating goose bumps to pebble my flesh. Nestling closer, I closed my eyes and gave in to the exhaustion I'd been fighting.

The movement of a body next to mine pulled me from a dirty dream. Stretching, I realized the warm body pressed against me was not a dream at all—it was Madison. Glancing at her body, melded to mine, I struggled to keep my hands off her skin. I could feel the curves hidden beneath the shirt she wore, making my morning wood throb with need.

She stretched, her leg rubbing against my erection. "Massimo?"

"Madison." I ran my hand through her hair, desperately trying to ignore my erection. "Did you sleep well?"

Jerking away from me when her leg bumped into the early morning surprise, she sat up. "Why are we in bed together?"

"You asked me to sleep here, remember?"

"Crap." She rubbed her eyes as she pulled the sheet over her body, clutching it beneath her neck. "I'm sorry. I shouldn't have done that."

I rolled to my side and propped myself onto my elbow. "Why? I can be a gentleman."

"I know. I just…" She shifted nervously. "We barely know each other, and… Well, there's the issue of you being my boss."

"It was innocent, Madison." I rolled away from her and stood beside the bed. "You were still upset about what happened at your apartment and needed to feel safe."

Even though I knew sleeping beside her changed everything for me, she needed time to accept the pull between us. Slowly making my way toward the bathroom, I glanced back at her. She was watching my every move, her knuckles white as she gripped the cotton fabric. "I'm going to shower, then we can discuss what to do from here."

I pushed the door closed some, leaving it slightly ajar in case she needed me. The protector in me needed to know she was always safe, even in my own home. I stripped off my boxers, turned on the water, and stepped beneath the hot stream. This woman had me all twisted up inside, and she probably didn't even know it. Bracing my hands against the cool tile, I let my head drop. The heat of the spray washed over me as the stall filled with steam. My mind couldn't stop thinking about Madison and the uncontrollable desire to keep her. She was going to fight me every step when she realized I wouldn't be letting her go back to that dump. She wasn't going to struggle on her own ever again—starting today.

Madison was just going to have to see it my way, like everyone else did. No one argued with what I wanted. I asked…, and they made it happen. This was no different. My father raised me to be a leader and to take what I wanted. Thinking about my father reminded me of the missing shipment. We knew it was the Sureños who'd intercepted the transport with the help of Jose Juarez, who was now dead.

Turning my head to stare at the cracked door, I could just barely see Madison standing beside the bed. Her dark hair fell around her shoulders like waves of chocolate silk. She had her dress laid out on the mattress. I wondered if she realized I could see her. My dick throbbed at the sight of her. Unable to stop myself, I reached down and fisted my shaft.

I couldn't see much of her, but what little I saw had me harder than I'd ever been. Trapped in utter fascination, I watched as she dropped my dress shirt to the floor, exposing her bare ass. I nearly lost my load, realizing she'd not been wearing any panties the entire night.

Closing my eyes, I tugged at my flesh. The desire to bury myself in her sweet pussy was overwhelming. When I opened my eyes, I noticed she was facing the door, but it appeared as though she didn't realize it was partially open—or that I was jacking off.

My fingers gripped my shaft hard as I slid my hand up and down. My free hand braced me against the glass as I watched her. Standing butt-ass naked, giving me a glorious view of her perfect breasts. They were round, with the most beautiful pink nipples. My balls tingled as I pumped faster. My head spun as my back tightened, signaling my release was close. Squeezing my eyes closed, I let myself go and groaned her name into the room.

The force of my ejaculation was unlike anything I'd ever felt before. My cum sprayed out of my cock, coating the glass partition as I let out a feral groan. My hand oozed with semen as I jerked the last of my orgasm from my body, nearly blacking out from its powerful force.

When I blinked open my eyes, my breath caught as I found the most beautiful blue eyes staring back.

She was standing in the doorway, clad in her black dress, her mouth agape as I held my hard cock in hand.

There was no doubt she'd seen me masturbating and why.

MADISON

HOLY. Mother. Fricken. Crap.

His thing was a monster.

I shouldn't have gone to the door.

I knew better.

I mean…it was the bathroom, but I was certain I heard him calling my name and was terrified to keep a man like him waiting. I might have only been in his apartment for twenty-four hours, but he wasn't someone to argue with.

Whatever he said was law, and no one went against him.

When I pulled open the door, I froze at the sight of him inside the giant glass enclosure. His muscular frame was bent beneath the rivulets of water dripping down his skin. The muscles of his back flexed as he worked himself with his hand. His head was tossed back, his eyes were pinched shut, and his lip was caught between his perfect white teeth.

I should have turned around, but I couldn't take my eyes off him—I couldn't. Massimo Anastasi might have been scary as fuck, but in this moment, he was a walking-talking porno.

My eyes tracked the evidence of his orgasm as it mixed with the drops of water and trailed down the thin barrier separating us. The sound of my name made me jerk my eyes to his face, which resembled a man lost to his dirty thoughts.

Had he just been jerking off to me? I sucked in a gasp at the realization my boss was masturbating while thinking of me, and I'd just stood there watching him.

His eyes popped open, his feral gaze pinning me to the spot. "Madison?" Massimo blinked, confused as to why I was standing in the doorway.

I jumped at his voice, looking up to meet his piercing dark gaze. "Um… I. Uh. Sorry." I sputtered my words, completely dumbstruck.

Hunger and heat filled his nearly black eyes as he stared at me like a juicy steak he wanted to devour. My world was spinning. The boss was calling my name, and instead of shame, I was overcome with so much desire that I didn't realize I should probably run away.

When I finally came to my senses, I bolted. Jerking the door closed, I ran to the kitchen. I was beyond mortified. I'd just seen my boss beating his meat like there was no tomorrow and heard my name cross his lips. I didn't know what to do with that.

At almost twenty-one, my sexual experience was a heavy make-out session with a boy from college. He wanted more, but I wasn't ready for that kind of commitment. So, there I stood—two feet away from the most glorious penis in the world—a virgin.

"Shoot," I muttered when I realized he'd probably seen me changing. Which meant I had definitely turned him on. That sent a thrill through my body instead of embarrassment. Grabbing a cup, I turned on the coffeemaker and waited. Maybe we could pretend it didn't happen.

What the heck was I going to say?

Oops, I didn't mean to walk in on you masturbating. Or how about the fact I stayed and watched?

God… The situation was all kinds of messed up.

"Madison."

I jumped at his voice, looking up to meet his piercing dark eyes. "Massimo." He was dressed in snug dark wash jeans, a red, fitted T-shirt, and a black blazer.

We stared at each other, the air charged with the unspoken words. Was he mad at what I'd done?

"I need to handle some business downstairs." He grabbed his cell phone from the charger and shoved it into his pocket.

"Okay. I should probably go back to my place and try to work on getting the door fixed."

He shook his head. "It's being taken care of. My brother will send someone over to fix your door. Until it's done, I'd appreciate it if you stayed here."

"Look…" I smiled. "I appreciate what you did for me last night, but I need to go home."

Stepping toward me, he ran his thumb across my jaw, pressing it into my bottom lip.

"Why are you still fighting me on this?"

I sighed when his hand dropped from my face. "You don't need to give me special treatment."

"I'm not." He smiled. "You're going to stay here until I know it's safe for you. I can't investigate the matter right now because of another pressing issue. Please do this for me. I couldn't live with it on my conscience if I let you go home, and you got hurt."

I mulled over his words. After everything he'd done for me in the last twelve hours, I didn't want to seem ungrateful. "Fine, but I want to go home soon. If your…" She furrowed her brow. "What is Donny? Your security?"

"Yes, you could call him that. He's also my best friend, and I trust him with my life."

"Well, the police said it would be nearly impossible to figure out who did this. You should call him off; it's a waste for him to look into this."

"That won't be necessary; it's his job to do what I ask." I watched as he scribbled something on a piece of paper. "Here's the access code for the elevator. I'd appreciate it if you didn't share it with anyone."

I looked at the slip and took it. "I won't. Will I see you today?"

"Of course." He headed toward the door. "I own the place, so being around is part of the job." He mashed his finger to the reader, making the elevator whirl to life. As the doors opened, he paused with his hand holding the metal doors from closing. "And Madison?" He called out to me.

"Yeah?" My eyes found his.

"My cock hasn't been that hard for anyone. Ever. Next time, I won't be coming in my hand." He slipped inside, and the doors slid shut.

My cheeks were on fire from embarrassment, but my panties were embarrassingly soaked with desire. I had to go back to my apartment soon, or I'd be making a mistake that involved my boss's penis inside me.

I couldn't afford to lose this job, but staying here was a stupid idea. I grabbed my satchel and hurried to the elevator. Keying in the code, I climbed inside and held my breath. I just needed some space to figure out what in the heck I was doing.

As soon as the elevator stopped at the bottom floor, I high-tailed to the front entrance. I knew if Massimo caught me leaving, he'd stop me. I'd just stepped outside when I slammed into a hard body.

"Ooof." A hand reached out and steadied me. "Fudge pickle." I glanced up to find the most frightening eyes glaring back and a hint of amusement tinting his lips.

"Where you running off to, little girl?" Vincenzo Anastasi stood on the sidewalk, looking at me like I was a criminal on the run. "Better yet... Does my brother know you're out here? Last I heard, he had you locked up there in his ivory tower."

A nervous giggle burst from my lips. "Yeah…sure. I'm just running to grab some things. I'll be back, excuse me." I moved out of his hold and stepped around his frame. He was just as large as Massimo, but somehow he was way scarier. "See ya round."

Like a scared rabbit, I practically ran—well, as much as I could in the heels I'd worn to work—down the street. By the time I reached my apartment building, I was panting hard. Climbing the steps, I wasn't at all surprised to find my door in the same state I'd left it in the night before. Blowing out a frustrated breath, I finagled it open and stepped inside.

Everything was in shambles, just as I remembered. Shaking off the worry, I headed to the tiny closet in my bathroom. I pulled out my old suitcase and began shoving things inside. Until the door got fixed, there was no way I was staying— and despite his pleas earlier, I wasn't staying at my boss's place either.

I paused for a moment, staring at the mess around me. The broken glass, the overturned furniture, the eerie silence that filled the room. My heart pounded in my chest, and I felt a niggle of fear wash over me. I had to get out of there to find some semblance of safety and control. I changed out of the dress I'd worn last night, tossing it to the floor. I quickly threw on some new panties and bra before grabbing a dress from my closet. The cotton material felt cool against my skin, a stark contrast to the tight material I'd had on. While slipping on my pink Converse, I took several steadying breaths.

I steadied my racing thoughts and continued packing, throwing in clothes, toiletries, and anything I could think of. I didn't even hear the door creak open or the heavy footsteps approaching.

"Madison."

eleven

MASSIMO

EVERYONE WAS GATHERED around my desk, trying to figure out what to do about the missing guns and Miguel Angel's proposition. Having him take over as the Sureños leader would be beneficial to us, but getting him there would be bloody.

Antonio shifted in his chair. "From what I found, the dead driver was definitely on Juan's payroll. I'm not sure why he felt the need to kill him and leave his body in Vin's alley, but there's definitely some kind of significance to it."

"I've got a couple of guys looking into the driver, and from what Alec was able to dig up on the computer, the little shit was in debt up to his eyeballs. You know money talks when you're desperate." Donny blew out a frustrated breath. "My concern is the guys are starting to get restless."

"Tell me about it. I've had three quit this morning. They're all afraid the Suerno's are going to off them." Antonio sighed, his weariness loud in the room.

Vincenzo finally arrived, his tardiness a new thing. "What'd I miss?"

"If you showed up on time, you'd know, fratello." My tone was that of his acting Don, not his brother. "This new version of you is not going to fly, Vin. You're my fucking second and you've been absent lately. I get you're going through some shit but you have a duty to the family, not your dick."

"So the little piece of ass you got stowed away in your apartment isn't a distraction?" He folded his arms across his chest. The surprise on my face made him smirk. "Yeah… I know all about you bringing her home last night. Though I gotta say she seemed pretty determined to get the hell away from here just now."

I blinked, surprised at his defiant attitude, but then his words registered. "What do you mean she was getting away?"

"You're little girl plowed into me on the sidewalk just now."

Pushing to my feet, I snapped, "Meetings over. Everyone out."

"Jesus, brother." Antonio stood. "You're ending a meeting because Madison went home?"

"I told her to stay put. Someone broke into her fucking apartment last night and until I know who, she wasn't to leave the casino."

I grabbed my cell phone and Ace of spades card I carried around and shoved them in my pocket and stormed out of the office. I was the acting Don, they could all kiss my ass right now because getting to Madison took top priority.

"Should we wait around for you?" Vincenzo joked as he practically ran behind me.

Stopping in my tracks, I spun to face him. "No. Get Miguel on the phone tell him we're ready to align with him—I'm done playing games with these motherfuckers."

With that I turned and marched out of the casino. Donny met me outside and followed me to the parked SUV. "I'll drive." He nodded toward the passenger side, "Get in."

He navigated us out onto the road, "Go easy on her, Massimo. She's not part of our world and you losing your shit is going to make her run the other way." He glanced my direction. "And if I'm right, you don't want that."

I grunted, "Shut up and just drive."

I hopped out of the car and took the steps to her apartment two at a time. The door, which barely hung on its frame, was ajar. I slipped inside and stood, watching Madison as she shoved things haphazardly into a bag. She'd changed into a gray T-shirt dress that hit midthigh. I stifled a laugh when I glanced down to find her tying the laces on a pair of bright pink converse high-tops. Everything about this girl was wrong for a man like me, but it didn't stop me from standing there wanting her.

"Madison."

My voice, laced with fury, broke through her reverie, and she stood quickly and spun around, her eyes wide with surprise. Her reaction made my blood boil even more. I could see the panic in her eyes, and it only fueled my anger.

What the hell do you think you're doing?" I growled, each word dripping with restrained fury. "Leaving my place, putting yourself at risk?"

"I-I just needed to grab some things…" Her voice faltered under my intense gaze, and she looked like a deer caught in headlights.

"You just needed to grab some things?" I repeated mockingly, stepping closer. "Do you understand how dangerous it is being here? I told you to stay put for a reason!"

She took a step back, her back hitting the edge of the bed. "You might be my boss, but you don't control my personal life…sir."

I ran a hand through my hair, frustration palpable. "You think this is about control? This is about keeping you safe!"

Tears pricked at the corners of her eyes, but she blinked them back, trying to stand her ground. "I can be safe in a hotel."

She turned to gather her things, and something inside me snapped. I stepped forward, grabbing her arm and spun her toward me. Without giving her a chance to react, I crashed my lips onto hers, kissing her hard. The kiss was fierce, fueled by anger, fear, and an undeniable attraction that neither of us could deny.

She stiffened for a moment, surprised, but then melted into me, her hands clutching at my shirt. My hand palmed her ass as I tugged her into my body and my free hand slipped around her throat. Tightening my hold, I walked her backward and pressed her back against the wall.

"You are driving me crazy." I pressed my lips against her ear, nipping at the tender flesh as I slid my palm down the front of her body. "I should let you go—but I can't, Bella." The endearment in Italian meant beautiful, a perfect term for the stunning woman in my hold.

My fingers gripped the cotton hem and I shoved her dress up, holding it beneath my palm as I tightened my fingers around her neck, the material bunched beneath my digits.t . Using my free hand I pull the black cotton bra down, exposing her breast before finally reaching between her legs. Before she could protest, I ripped the flimsy panties from her body and brushed my fingers through her curls and shoved them between her folds. "Fuck." I groaned at the feel of her warmth. "You're soaking for me baby." Her eyes closed as she pulled her lip between her teeth. Unable to stop myself, I suck at the tender flesh of her neck, taking what I want.

Madison whimpered as I drove my fingers in deeper, her body tensing briefly from the sudden intrusion. "You're so tight." Her body tensed and her fingers dug into my shoulder.

"Massimo." My name came out as a breathy moan. "I—oh."

"Do you like my finger's buried inside your pretty pussy?"

Her breaths came out in pants as I worked her body. I covered her mouth with mine just as her body tightened around my digits and she cried out. The way her body quaked in my hold was better than anything I'd ever experienced myself and I couldn't wait to feel that sensation wrapped around my cock.

Her head fell forward against my shoulder, her breaths came out in pants as she came down from the orgasmic high. I steadied her on her feet and adjusted her dress. When she lifted her head I couldn't resist and pressed my lips against hers.

"You're coming home with me, Madison." I turned and grabbed her bag. "Let's go, Bella."

Before she could respond, I shoved open her door and stepped into the hallway. Donny was leaned against the wall outside her door waiting. There was no doubt he heard Madison, but he wouldn't dare say anything to embarrass her.

Madison stepped out of her apartment. "I'm ready."

As we sat in the back of my car, the silence between us felt heavy. Madison stared out the window, her fingers nervously fidgeting with the hem of her dress. I was dying to understand what was going on in her mind, but the constant glances she kept shooting toward Donny told me she was embarrassed to talk in front of him.

Donny was in the driver's seat, eyes on the road, but I knew he could hear us. Madison's hesitation was palpable. I leaned closer, lowering my voice even further. "If you're worried about him, don't be. "Madison, anything you tell me stays between us. Donny won't say anything."

She looked down at her hands, her voice trembling when she spoke. "I'm not upset, Massimo."

Her admission was a relief but didn't do much to alleviate my concern. If she wasn't upset, then what was it that had been eating at her since we left her place? I had to know.

"Then why are you so quiet?" I asked, trying to keep my tone gentle despite the irritation I was feeling.

She bit her lip, clearly struggling with something. I wasn't at all prepared for what she said.

"Massimo, I'm a virgin," she blurted out, her cheeks flushing with embarrassment. "I've never done anything like that before."

"You're a *virgin*?" The shock was impossible to hide. I knew she was innocent, but not to this extent. For fuck's sake, Madison was beautiful. How had she gone this long and never been touched? Surely men had tried to bed her. "How is this possible?"

Her brows furrowed as she looked down at her lap. "I mean —I haven't exactly put myself out there. Bouncing from foster home to foster home meant I wasn't anywhere long enough to have a boyfriend. And when I started college, I focused all my attention on surviving and getting good grades."

"Fuck, bella." I growled, tugging her hand from its coiled position on her lap. "What we just did—I wouldn't have touched you had I known. Not like that. I'm sorry if I pressured you or made you uncomfortable."

She shook her head quickly. "No, you didn't. I wanted to… I just didn't know how to tell you. Everything happened so fast, and I was too embarrassed to tell you to stop."

"Never be afraid to tell me to anything, bella." I pressed my lips against her knuckles. "This changes things between us."

She stiffened beside me. "Are you going to fire me?"

I couldn't help the laugh that bubbled out. "No, Bella. But things will be different."

"Different how?" She lifted her gaze to mine, the vulnerability in her eyes made me want to pull her across the seat and hold her against my body.

"Because now you're mine."

"I don't—" She turned her head to the window. "What does that mean, exactly?"

"It means you belong to me, Madison."

She shifted uncomfortably beside me. "I'm not a possession, Massimo. Just because you…touched me doesn't mean you suddenly own me. Heck, twenty-four hours ago you barely tolerated me at work."

"You're wrong, Madison. I acted that way because I wanted something I shouldn't." I shifted to press my lips against her ear and whispered, "But now that I've had my fingers inside that tight little pussy, I'm not stopping myself from taking everything from you." I brushed my thumb across the pulse in her throat. "And I am man who gets what he wants."

"That's the problem." She cut her eyes toward me. "I'm the last woman you should want; I'm a nobody and you are… someone."

The car stopped at the front of the Velvet Ace and Madison bolted from the car before I can stop her. I start after her, but Antonio steps in my path. "We have a problem."

I moved to go around him, but he grabbed my arm. "I hope you have a damn good reason for stopping me like this, because if not…" I narrowed my gaze on my younger brothers face, "I won't hesitate to put a bullet in your head— brother or not."

Antonio glanced toward the entrance where Madison disappeared through, "I get it—you want to chase after her, but something happened at Vin's restaurant. Something that could fuck up our deal with Miguel."

"Fuck." I swiped my palm down my face. "Fine. Let's go."

I turned around and motioned for Donny to get back into the car. Antonio climbed in the back and as we headed out of the parking lot, I sent Carlisle a text message telling him to ensure Madison got into my apartment safely. Aside from my family, and a few of the security guys at the casino, he was the only one with access to my elevator.

"What the fuck happened?" I shoved my phone inside my jacket pocket. My level of irritation was beyond nuclear. I looked at my brother and finally noticed the strain in his face.

"Miguel's sister was murdered." He held my gaze. "And left inside Vin's office."

twelve

MASSIMO

WHEN I STEPPED into The Sapphire Dagger, I knew the situation was beyond fucked. My brother sat in his office chair, a blade flipping between his fingers as he stared at the body laid out in front of him. The staff had all been told not to come in, and the restaurant had been closed for the night "due to a busted water line."

His eyes were trained on her body as if he was caught in some kind of memory from his past. So, not only did I have to deal with my brother's fucked up mental state, I had to figure out why Miguel Angel's sister was lying across the surface of his desk.

"Vin," I called out as I stood at the entrance to his office. "Fratello, can you talk to me?"

His eyes flicked up to mine. "Massimo?" His gaze traveled back to her still frame. "I didn't do this. I—" He leaned back in his chair and sighed. "She was shot between the eyes. They left this." He held up a heart-shaped locket.

I didn't need him to tell me. Not only was it evident from the massive portion of her head missing, but my brother had a very specific calling card. Whoever left her here obviously didn't do their research—or it was merely a message.

"Why would they do this?" He waved his hand toward her. "She was tortured, Massimo. *Tortured.* They fucking tied her up like a goddamn dog, stripped her naked, and—*fuck!*" he bellowed into the room.

"Ana!" Miguel's bellow echoed through the empty restaurant. "Get out of my way!" His thick Spanish accent filled the nearly empty restaurant.

Knowing he did not need to see this, I stepped out and stood in front of him. "No. Miguel, you do not need to see this— your sister wouldn't want you to remember her like this."

"Fuck you, puta." He tried to shove me aside, but I wrapped my arms around his waist. "Get the fuck off me, or I'll put a bullet in your head, gringo."

"Listen to him, Miguel." Vincenzo stood in the doorway. "You don't want to have this burned into your memory. I've seen and done plenty of things, but this—" he shook his head, "is fucked up. Your sister has been humiliated—her body broken in ways that make me want to set fire to the world for you."

The formidable man crumbled in my arms. His body was wracked with sobs. "She was all I had left." He pushed me back, stumbling from my hold. "Who did this? My sister was a beautiful creature. She did not deserve the death she was given."

"None of my men had anything to do with it. This—" I waved to the office, "is a declaration of war."

"You're damn right it is." Miguel wiped his face. "Are you with me now, Mr. Anastasi? Do you see how easily it is for Juan to take what he wants—no regard for women? He wants me to lash out and kill you. But his mistake was choosing this place to leave her. Even I know La Lama wouldn't blow my sister's brains out. No..." his eyes sought my brothers, "you prefer to leave a more personal statement, don't you?"

"I don't know what you're talking about." Vincenzo lifted his chin. "And it's in your best interest to watch your tongue. La Lama is a ghost... Best to leave him there."

"You think I chose your family because of your hold on weapons? Or the power you wield here in Vegas?" Miguel spat on the floor near my feet. "No! I chose you because of a ghost. So I will ask you again," he pinned me with a glare, "are you with me?"

"We're with you." I nodded. "Time to go hunting. Donny, get some guys together."

"Yes, sir." He turned and hurried out of the hallway.

"Vin." I turned to my brother; the haunted look in his eyes worried me. "We need someone here to dispose of her body. She deserves to be laid to rest like a person. Can you manage that?"

"Of course." He started to head back into his office but paused, "Miguel, I swear on my life, when Juan is brought in, he'll be seeing ghosts of his own."

"Thank you." Miguel paused. It was obvious he was torn about whether or not he should go and confirm it was his sister. Instead, he flicked his eyes to me. "You're sure it's my Ana?"

Vin held out the golden trinket, "This was with her." He dropped the necklace into Miguel's hand before disappearing inside.

"I'm going to gut every person who helped him do this."

My men spent the next several hours cleaning up the body left behind by Juan. He'd made his statement, and now, we would make ours. Under the cover of night, my men would find him and bring him to us. We would make sure his last breath would be painful. This was no longer about stealing from my family; it was about crossing the line when he killed Miguel's sister.

Nodding, "When they pick him up, they'll bring him to the Casino. I'll call you when it happens."

Miguel turned and stormed out of The Sapphire Dagger. His sister was a casualty of the festering war Juan Carlos started when he took something of mine. He always seemed to be one step ahead of us, but not anymore. We were going to bring the fight to him. Donny and Antonio waited outside for me.

"Father called." Antonio's voice held an edge to it that I recognized all too well. "He has called me to Italy. I asked him for a couple of days to help sort this out with you, but I'll be leaving in three days." Of the six children, he would take Grandfather's death the hardest as he and grandfather were the closest out of the six children.

I squeezed his shoulder. "I know. He and I spoke. And while I might be the Don here in Vegas, he is all of our leader. I wish I could join you, but I'm needed here."

Antonio nodded.

"I'm worried about Vin."

"We can't think about that right now, Antonio. We can only hope this doesn't set his recovery back." I sighed. We came close to losing Vincenzo when his demons became too much for him. "Perhaps we should encourage him to visit Onyx."

The club gave him a way to express himself without putting anyone, especially himself, in danger. "Yeah…maybe."

The ride back to the Velvet Ace was tense. When we pulled in, Antonio headed to his car.

Stepping into the lounge, I scanned the room for Madison. I wasn't stupid. I knew she'd decided to work. Carlisle had texted me, saying she had shown up downstairs for her shift. When I didn't immediately spot her, I headed to the bar where Carlisle was standing.

"Carlisle." His head jerked toward me. "Where is Madison?"

He held my gaze a moment longer than I liked. "Sir…she's ah…" he swallowed nervously. Maddie's in one of the private rooms."

Shooting my hand out across the surface of the bar, I grabbed his shirt and tugged him across. "What the fuck did you just say?"

Carlisle closed his eyes as he repeated his words. "She's in back, sir. Julie has the flu, so Maddie offered to fill in for her."

"Are you fucking stupid? You *let* my girlfriend work a private party—who the fuck has the room tonight?"

"Um." Confusion marred his expression, hearing me call Madison mine. He licked his lips nervously before responding. "The district attorney."

"You've gotta be fucking kidding me." I shoved him away. "Not only did you send her to a *private* party without consulting me...you sent her to the worst fucking group there is."

I wasn't mad because she was back there, per se. I knew Carlisle wouldn't have sent her to work a private party if he didn't think she couldn't handle it.

No.

I was mad because I knew what went on with some of the groups —the district attorney being the worst of them. They all thought they were above the law and did what they pleased. A few of my girls didn't mind the extra attention because it resulted in extra tips, but I didn't want anyone else's hands on her—she was *mine.*

Pissed off, I rushed down the hallway. Two of my security guys noted my rage and hurried to catch up. I'm sure they thought something was wrong based on my expression. Not to mention, they'd just witnessed me tossing Carlisle to the side.

Madison's soft voice filtered through the silent room. "Look, you need to let me go before this escalates."

"Baby, I want it to escalate." He ground his body into hers, causing her dress to ride up her body. A body that belonged to me. I watched as she tried to wiggle free from him again. "Oh, you like it rough, do you?"

I'd never felt the urge to put a bullet in a man's head quite like I did the moment I stepped into the private room. When I pushed open the door and saw the assistant district attorney, Chris Patterson, with his hands on her, all rational thought flew out the window. The motherfucker had Madison by her throat and pressed up against the wall. Her fingers were clawing at his forearms in an effort to free herself. Her scared gaze snapped to mine, her glazed eyes moments away from spilling tears.

"What the fuck is going on?".

Patterson turned his disgusting head toward me. "Mr. Anastasi," Patterson smirked as he leaned forward and licked her neck, making her whimper.

In two strides, I was across the room, my gun pulled free of its holster. I pressed the cool metal barrel against his head. "Take your fucking hands off her."

Patterson let go of her throat and pushed his hands into the air. "Whoa, Anastasi. Calm down."

"I'll calm down when you move away from her. Madison," I held out my hand, "come here." I could see the resolve slowly crumbling in her gaze. "If one fucking tear falls from her eyes, you're going to be eating a bullet." Tugging her hand, I pushed her behind me. Madison pressed her body to my back, my palm pressing her firmly in place.

"She's just another fucking piece of pussy, Anastasi." Patterson scoffed. "I'm sure it isn't any good anyway."

The sound of my gun echoed throughout the space. His brain coated the paint as his body crumpled to the ground. Madison squeaked as she buried her face into the back of my jacket.

"What the fuck? You fucking shot him!" Mike Donovan, his boss and the Vegas district attorney, said in disbelief.

"Party is over. Get your people out of here." Madison began to shake violently against me before turning and vomiting on the floor. I didn't stop to think when I put a bullet in that fucker's head, but seeing her like that pissed me off even more. Turning, I pulled her against my front, burying her head against my chest. "Locke," I called over to one of my guys, "call Donny and tell him we need a clean-up crew."

"You're making a mistake, Anastasi. You just murdered a man in front of me." Donovan stepped forward, his face a mask of rage. "You won't get away with this."

Shifting my gun, I pointed it at his head. "And I'll put a bullet between your eyes, too, Donovan. You don't scare me. What would the higher-ups in this community think if I showed them some footage from Onyx?" His eyes widened in shock. "That's right, Donovan. I record everything in this place. *Everything.*"

His face paled. "What the fuck? Are you threatening me?"

"Take it as you will. All I know is I walked in on your guy," I pointed at the dead man whose blood was staining my carpet, "trying to force himself on *my* girl. People have died for less."

I shoved my gun into the holster and scooped Madison into my arms. "Get out, Donovan. Figure out how you'll spin this, or you'll be the next one with lead poisoning."

I turned and carried Madison from the room. Carlisle glanced toward us, his eyes widening with concern. I'd deal with him later, but Madison needed my attention more. She didn't speak as we stepped into the elevator, nor on the ride up to my apartment.

I knew she suspected certain things about me, but seeing is believing. This was going to be an awkward conversation, but I needed her to trust me.

The only way for that to happen was to tell her *everything*.

thirteen

MADISON

EVERY SINGLE NERVE ending was firing with anger and confusion. Obviously, the hushed rumors about him were true—he'd just killed a man in front of me. A man who, in his own right, was a monster. If Massimo hadn't stepped into that room when he had, I have no doubt the assistant district attorney would have raped me.

And that thought made my stomach churn with bile. "Who are you, really?" I could hardly look at him as he set me down on my feet.

His shoulders drooped as he huffed and headed into the kitchen. I watched as he pulled down two glasses and poured whiskey into each of them. Carrying them over to the couch, he motioned to the cushion beside him.

"Sit."

I hesitated, wanting to defy his request, but was too over-whelmed with everything else to even bother. My head was still reeling from the fact I'd just watched him murder a man downstairs like it was nothing. I took the seat at the opposite end, away from him. Leaning down, I slipped off my high heels, rubbing at the redness from being on my feet all day. Shock rolled through me when Massimo scooted closer and set the tumblers on the coffee table, then reached down and tugged my feet into his lap.

"I'm going to tell you everything because I want you to trust me." He began to knead my sore muscles, causing my eyes to close and hiss to escape my lips. "But… I'm going to need something from you first."

I opened my eyes. "Something from me?"

"What I'm about to tell you could place you and my family in danger. I need to have your loyalty."

"Or what? You'll kill me?" I said in a mocking tone, but his body language told me I wasn't too far off from the truth. "Holy crap balls…you will!"

"I'm hoping I can earn *your* loyalty…maybe even more." He dug his fingers into the sole of my foot, hitting the spot that ached. "You've met my brothers, but what you don't know is. My family is one of the oldest crime syndicates in Vegas. My father, Giacomo Anastasi, came here with my mother before we were born. He built an empire on his own. Now, we're one of the most feared families in the area. The businesses are all part of the empire my dad built."

He continued his ministrations on my feet, his hand working some kind of magic on my muscles. "We have a lot of government officials in our pocket. The club has helped increase that number. They come here to let loose and do things that most would frown upon. Onyx is a place where they can be someone else. And that gives us leverage."

"People can buy a membership at Onyx or pay a lot of money for one of the private rooms—like the one you were in tonight. They know they can do whatever they want—within reason—behind the locked doors, and we don't interfere."

"How does that give you leverage?"

"Everything is recorded." He held my gaze.

"Wait, you're telling me you can watch what happens in the club?"

He took a breath. "Yes, but I don't. I only review the cameras when needed."

"For blackmail."

"Yes. I'm not a saint, Madison."

I slipped my legs off him and stood. Walking to the window overlooking the Vegas skyline, I crossed my arms. Even after everything he told me, I still felt safer in his care than anywhere else. He hadn't admitted to doing other illegal things per se, but gathering blackmail on government officials told me he probably did. Plus, I wasn't ignorant of what the mafia was. I'd read enough growing up to know they were a real organization, not just made up for television.

"I'll understand if you no longer want to work for me. You don't have to be afraid to leave. I'd never hurt you."

"Why? What makes me so special?" I continued to stare out the window.

"Everything."

Turning to look at him, I watched him as he sat with his elbows on his knees and his head hung. He looked defeated as if he was waiting for me to stomp all over his heart.

My eyes flicked to the holster still strapped to his body. "I'm not used to this life, and you scare me with your overbearing ways." I turned and looked out the massive window overlooking Vegas. The night lights glittered in the black sky, casting a luminous glow over the city. "I hate violence, Massimo. After my mother—god… You shot a man tonight." My tears finally fell as a sob tore from my lips.

"I'm not sorry for reacting the way I did. He shouldn't have been touching you, and it's not the first time he's pushed himself on one of my employees." He pressed a kiss to the exposed skin on my shoulder. "I'm only sorry you had to witness it."

"I don't know if I can live like this, Massimo." I swiped at my tears. My eyebrow quirked. "Would you have reacted that way had I been anyone else?"

Massimo stood quietly for a moment. "No, I wouldn't have reacted so…*violently.*"

"Why is that Massimo? I'm no one special."

"Sometimes, when you meet someone," his unwavering gaze seemed to peer into my soul. You know they're your anima gemelli."

"Anima Gemelli?"

"Italian for soul mate."

My heart pounded. I wanted to deny what he said, but there was a magnetic pull between us that made me want to believe, even a little, that maybe he was right. "I see."

"I don't expect you to feel the same yet." Massimo leaned across and cupped my cheek. "But if you give me a chance, you'll see the truth in my words."

I leaned into his palm, the warmth of his skin melding into mine. Everything about him called to me as though he was the siren and I was the sailor. "I think I should go home."

His thumb traced my skin. "You are home, bella."

"You know what I mean, Massimo. I have an apartment."

"Not anymore. Donny took care of the broken door, but he learned your landlord has been stealing the money renters give him. You can't go back. What little you left behind has been packed up and will be delivered tomorrow, along with some other things I've picked out for you."

"This is moving too fast…" I stood and paced the room. "I need some time. Jeepers, Massimo. You decided how my life would go without even considering how I would feel."

"I don't want to waste time, bella." He shrugged his shoulders. "Things are changing for my family, and I need my personal life to move along for the sake of those changes."

He shoved his hands into his pockets and rocked back on his heels. "My grandfather has taken ill, and my father will be officially taking his place sooner rather than later. I've been acting as the head of my family—but…" He leaned against the counter, watching me.

"Your father, the *Don*?"

Massimo chuckled at my question. "Yes...the Don."

"You're going to be taking over for real."

"Yes." He smiled like what he was telling me wasn't crazy. "I have been groomed since I was old enough to understand what my family was to take over one day. That day has come."

"You're going to be over...all this?" I waved my hand through the air as if his apartment held the keys to his kingdom.

"Yes. Does that frighten you?"

I moved into the kitchen, my mind racing a thousand thoughts. After grabbing a bottle of water from the refrigerator, I unscrewed the lid and took a large gulp. Between the crying, throwing up, and the explosion of the gun, my head was pounding.

"I don't really understand enough to be frightened. All I've ever heard about the mafia, I learned from TV or from the rumors I've heard at school. Is it like that?"

"To an extent, yes. With less murder, though." I opened the pantry as he moved in behind me, the heat of his body washing over me as his lips pressed beside my ear when he spoke. "What are you looking for?"

Trying to hide the blush creeping up my skin, I ducked my head. "Sorry, I'm a little hungry. I was trying to find something to eat."

"Let me call downstairs. Someone can run and get us food."

I shook my head. "It's almost eleven. I'll be fine."

"I won't. I haven't eaten today." Massimo pulled his cell out and called down to the bar. After telling them what he wanted, I watched as he put his phone on the charger. "Dinner will be here in an hour. How about you take a bath? It'll be good for your muscles. Is there something particular you'd like to eat?"

I sighed, feeling the tension in my shoulders melt away. "Anything is fine, and a bath sounds divine."

He extended his hand toward me. "Here, let me help you." When our hands met, mine fit perfectly in his. He led me gently into the bathroom. "Sit," he instructed, pointing to the lounger beside the tub. I watched as he turned on the water, added bath salts and bubbles, and tested the temperature. "All right, I'll be right outside if you need me," he said.

Before leaving, he leaned down and pressed a tender kiss on my head. I removed my dress and threw it on the floor; it felt like it was burning on my skin. I just wanted the day to be over. Stretching my arms, I sunk down into the overflowing bubbles. I kept seeing the man's head explode right in front of me. A part of me linked it to my mother's murder; the other part of me felt—flattered. How could I have such mixed emotions about something I abhorred? I swore that I'd never allow violence into my life again, and yet the man outside the bathroom stood for the one thing I hated most, and I still wanted him.

Reaching for the bottle of soap, my arm connected with the shampoo and sent it clattering to the floor.

"Crud." I tried to reach out to grab it, but it rolled out of my grasp.

"Madison?" Massimo tapped on the door as he eased it open to peer inside. "Everything all right?"

"Yeah, I'm sorry. I knocked over the shampoo, trying to grab it." I sunk beneath the bubbles, suddenly shy in front of him.

His gaze flicked to the tub before landing on my face. "Okay, I'll leave you be. I just wanted to make sure you were all right."

"Actually…" I hesitated. "Can you come inside and get the bottle? It rolled out of my reach, and I don't want to get out."

I watched as he pressed his head against the door and took a deep breath. Shoving from the door frame, he stepped inside. As he squatted beside the porcelain tub, his eyes darkened with desire. My arms were draped over the edge of the tub, a small hint of cleavage peeking out from beneath the suds. Shaking himself out of his haze, he picked up the runaway bottle.

"Here." His fingers brushed against mine, sending an electric shock through my body.

"Massimo," I whispered, feeling a spark ignite between us.

He dropped to his knees beside me and tugged me to the edge. His hand wound through my hair as he pulled my lips against his. I melted into him, our mouths moving in tune with each other. The water splashed out, wetting his shirt, and snapping him from the lustful moment.

"Madison." He pulled away. "We need to stop."

I nodded, embarrassment coursing through my entire being. "I'm sorry."

Tipping my chin up, he looked into my eyes. "Don't be. I just don't want to push you too fast like I did earlier."

My eyes blinked in shock. "You still want me?"

He gripped the edge, his knuckles going white. "More than my next breath, but I need you to be sure you want me too." Pushing back, he stood up. "I'll be outside. Dinner should be here any minute."

He'd barely made it to the door when I pushed myself to a stand. Hearing the water splash, he turned. His eyes roamed my body as I stood before him, the water and suds trickling down my bare flesh.

"What are you doing?" he asked, frozen, unable to move.

"I'm sure about what I want." I pressed my shoulders back, pushing my ample breasts out on display.

He inched toward me. "And what do you want, Madison?"

I climbed out and took a timid step toward him. "You… I want you."

Just as he moved to pull me into his arms, his phone buzzed in his pocket.

"Fuck." He jerked his phone out, his eyes locked with mine as he answered. "What?" He rubbed the bridge of his nose. "Okay, I'll buzz you up. Looks like dinner is here. I'll meet you in the living room." He turned and stormed out.

I was left stunned and very, *very* naked.

MADISON

DINNER ARRIVED at the worst possible moment. I finally convinced myself to tell him what I was feeling, then he had to go and answer that dang call. I dried off, then toweled my hair. I forgot my bag once again and contemplated walking out there naked just to torture him, but I wasn't that strong of a girl. Even doing what I had already took more guts than my inexperienced self was truly prepared for. After stepping out, draining the tub, and toweling off, I went in search of something to wear.

I sifted through his closet and snagged one of his button-down dress shirts. Rolling the sleeves up, I gave myself a once over in the mirror, then walked out. The elevator doors were closing, telling me whoever had delivered the food was already gone. Massimo had his back to me, and he was setting the food on the bar.

I paused, taking in his perfect physique. His jeans sculpted his backside perfectly, making my mouth water. The shirt he had on molded against his muscles, leaving me wanting to trace the defined ridges with my tongue. Whoa…where had that come from? I wasn't that girl. Heck, my experience was *very* limited.

Glancing toward the coffee table, I noticed he'd removed his gun. A moment of panic filled my chest, but I pushed it aside. If I wanted this man the way I thought I did, I couldn't let my past fears dictate the here and now.

"I hope you're hungry." He turned and started toward me before stopping dead in his tracks. "*Fuck…*"

He dropped the fork he was holding and stalked toward me. Stopping inches from me, he ran his fingers through my damp hair and down my arm. "I fucking love seeing you in my shirt."

"I hope you don't mind that I borrowed it," I whispered, uncertainty lacing my tone. I let my eyes roam over his chest. My insides throbbed with need, making the place between my thighs slick with desire. I'd forgone panties, hoping to pick up where we left off in the tub. I was a virgin, as he knew from earlier. And though my limited experiences with the opposite sex were nothing compared to what we'd done in my apartment, I knew what I wanted. Seeing him looking at me with hunger in his eyes made me want to do things I'd never done before.

"Not at all, bella." He ran his hand down my cheek, then trailed his finger across my collarbone where the shirt was open.

I gasped at the sensations pulsing beneath his touch. "Keep making those noises, and dinner will be forgotten." His hand tugged my hip, pulling me against him. I could feel the desire hidden beneath his zipper, making me bite my lip.

"Can it be reheated?" I bit my lip, my voice shy as I spoke.

"*Fuck*," he whispered before crashing his lips to mine.

Gripping my sides, he plundered my mouth. His tongue flicked against mine, drawing another moan from my throat. Massimo wedged his body between my legs as he ravished me with his intense kiss. Our tongues fought for dominance, the sexual tension bursting from our bodies as he backed me through the open floor plan and toward the bed. My legs hit the edge, stopping our movement. Massimo tugged at the shirt and paused as if seeking permission.

I reached between us and pulled it over my head.

"Goddamn it." He stepped back and drank me in. "Beautiful."

Slipping his hand between my legs, he pressed his fingers into my opening. I cried out, clenching my thighs together at the invasion. "Fuck, I'd almost forgotten how tight your sweet pussy was." He hissed as my pussy clamped down on his fingers like a vise. "That's it, bella, take it from me… take it all."

"Massimo., I cried out as an orgasm washed over me. Embarrassed by the quick release, I wouldn't look at his face.

"Madison." He tilted my chin up, his gaze laden with tenderness. "You don't need to hide from me."

"I don't think I will please you like you're used to." I ducked my head again, terrified of what he would say when he learned I had zero experience with sex

Stilling against me, his silence was deafening, and I almost pulled away. "Because you're a virgin," he said. "That doesn't matter. I'll teach you how to please me, bella."

"Yes, sir," I whispered the word, knowing things were about to change for us.

"Christ." He laid me down gently, then tugged his shirt over his head. "Look at me." I glanced at him through hooded eyes. "Never be embarrassed to tell me what you want or if I am going too fast. I'll have to get you ready to take my cock, pretty girl. I'm a big guy and don't want to hurt you." He shoved his pants down, taking his underwear with them. Before I could catch a glimpse of his dick, he covered my body with his massive frame as he ground his rock-hard erection between my legs, proving his point. "I need words, bella."

A moan mixed with my words slipped out. "I trust you."

"Good…" He slowly kissed his way down my belly. "Because I've been dying to taste you."

"Taste me?" I gasped, watching him as he positioned himself between my thighs.

"I want to know everything that makes your body burn for me." He swirled his finger around my clit. "Do you like it when I do this?"

"Yes," I moaned, bucking my hips against him. "Frick."

He slipped a finger inside my channel. "And this?"

"Oh, *Fraggle Rock*…" I groaned as my walls spasmed around his knuckle. My fingers gripped the satin sheets beneath me.

"Massimo." I whimpered his name, needing something but not sure what.

He grinned from between my legs, "You're something else, baby. Let go—you can even talk dirty, bella." He pushed his tongue in and out, scissoring his fingers inside me as his free hand gripped his cock. I was tight and worried he wouldn't fit, but I knew I wanted him to try. Shoving his tongue between my folds, he lapped at my center, getting it wet and ready to take all of him. Watching him jerk himself off as he ate me was the hottest thing I'd ever seen.

"So. Fucking. Sweet." He lifted his face from my pussy. "Are you ready for me to bury my cock inside you, bella?"

"Please, sir."

I was seconds away from losing my virginity to the most powerful man in Vegas. I should have been terrified, but instead, I was desperate for him to take me. Spreading my legs, I made room for his body as he climbed onto the bed. He propped himself up on his hands, his cock jutting out and dripping with pre-cum. I watched in fascination as he covered his erection with a condom and lined up against my opening.

Holy Crap. This was it...this was the moment everything changed.

"This will hurt at first, but once you've adjusted to me, I promise it will feel good."

"Okay," I whispered, holding his gaze in mine.

Reaching between us, he fisted his cock in his hand and eased it between my folds. I'd stolen another glance at his penis when he moved up the bed toward me, seeing it again confirmed what I'd already known—he was huge.. I was worried he wouldn't fit, but now, with his tip buried inside, I didn't care, and wanted more.

"Please," I mewled, wanting him to just bury himself inside me.

Smiling, Massimo pressed his lips to mine as he thrust inside. He burst through my barrier, tearing my innocence away in one quick motion. Pain shot through my body as he seated himself inside me, causing me to wince.

"Are you all right?" he asked, searching my face for pain.

I squeezed my eyes shut, trying to catch my breath. "Give me a minute."

He pressed kisses to my face, trailing down my jaw and settling his lips on my neck. Licking and sucking, he kept himself perfectly still inside me, waiting until I was ready for more. As quick as the pain appeared, it was replaced with something else—something almost feral.

I needed to feel him move.

"Please move."

Pulling him with my legs, I urged him to thrust his hips. It was a feeling of pure bliss, and when he pumped...holy mother of pearl, my body awoke with a fire that only he could sate.

His movements became harder and more demanding, begging for something I needed him to give. Every fiber in my body was lit with an electrical current I couldn't contain. The tingling started in my feet and traveled until it settled between my legs. I pushed my hips up, meeting him with every thrust. The friction from our coupling sent me careening over the edge. My orgasm coiled and snapped like a wound rubber band. I couldn't stop the scream coming from my mouth as my pussy contracted around his cock. Wetness gushed out between my legs as he pounded into me.

"Fuck…" he grunted, his movements becoming erratic. "I'm going to come."

He moaned into my ear as he tugged the flesh between his teeth. I didn't think it was possible to orgasm twice my first time, but the harder he slammed into me, the more my body responded. The familiar coiling started in my belly as his diamond-hard shaft slipped in and out of me.

"I can't hold off. I'm going to explode, baby. You ready?" He kissed me with desperation. "I need your tight little pussy to suck my cock dry. Can you do that for me, bella?"

"Oh, Gosh." A switch was flipped in my brain at his dirty words. "Yes, I'm coming, Massimo!"

We fell off the cliff together. My walls spasmed around his swollen member, milking his seed dry. He roared into the room as he drilled into my core, spilling inside the latex barrier. Warmth filled me as the condom swelled with his essence.

Massimo was breathing hard as he rolled off the top of me. His dick slipped from between my folds. The rubber coated in my blood was proof of our union.

"Jesus Christ. What was that?"

I furrowed my brow, worried I'd done something wrong. "What do you mean?"

"Mi hai distrutto per tutti gli altri," he mumbled into the pillow.

"What did you say? I don't speak Italian."

"I said you destroyed me for all others." Massimo rolled over to face me. "You're mine now. You understand that, don't you?"

MASSIMO

"YOURS? LIKE PROPERTY?"

"No, like my woman. Mine to protect. Mine to cherish."

She glanced at me, staring at my body as though it was edible. Her eyes trailed down, spotting the evidence of what we'd done as I removed the condom.

"Holy crap…I still can't believe that was inside me. She seemed shocked at how perfectly I'd fit inside her.

"You were made for me, bella." I chuckled at the way her eyes filled with hunger. It was a far cry from the haunted look earlier that night. "Are you hungry?"

"Yes, you've worked up my appetite." She leaned up, smiling. "That was," she pressed a kiss to my chest, "amazing. Thank you."

"Don't thank me yet. After dinner, I plan to take you again until you can't walk without remembering I was buried inside you. I want to imprint myself on your soul, so you'll never want to leave."

"I almost want to skip dinner." As if on cue, her stomach growled, making her giggle. "Guess food is in order instead."

"Wait here." I rolled out from under her and disposed of the condom. "I'll grab a towel to clean you off." After wiping the remnants of her release from the inside of her legs, I pulled her to her feet. "How does naked dinner sound, followed by my cock for dessert?" I waggled my eyebrows at her, causing her to blush.

She sauntered toward the counter, her hips swaying seductively. My eyes trailed behind her. Her ass was perfectly round, topping off the most luscious legs I'd ever seen. Seeing her stand there as naked as the day she was born caused my cock to stir again. I had a feeling I was going to have a permanent erection anytime she was around. It was a good thing she liked my cock, since I had a feeling she'd be seeing it often.

We'd barely finished eating the cold leftovers when my phone chimed. Glancing at the screen, I winced. "I'm sorry, bella. But I'm going to have to take care of something."

I stood and walked around to stand beside her. Pressing a kiss to her neck, I pulled her naked body against my own. " Get some sleep. When I come back, I'll wake you with my tongue buried here—" I pushed a finger between her wet folds.

"Where are you going?" Her words were breathy as I continued to play with her pussy.

Nipping at her ear, I said, "Business calls."

Stepping away from her, I held my hand out. "Come—let's get you into bed."

She glanced at the remnants of our meal, "What about—"

"Don't worry about the mess, Madison." I led her to the bed I'd just been tangled with her in and helped her crawl in. "I'll be back as soon as I can, bella."

I could tell she wanted to ask questions, but she simply nodded. "Okay. Be careful."

"Always. Plus," I cupped her breast in my palm, "I have something important waiting for me at home."

I pulled the sheet over her body and stepped back, feeling a heavy weight settle in my chest. The room felt cold, and the silence was deafening. Hurrying to the bathroom, I tried to shake off the dread that clung to me. The hot water cascaded over me as I showered quickly, but it did little to wash away the sense of something more was coming. Dressing in a suit, my hands trembled slightly, betraying my calm exterior.

When I emerged from the bathroom, Madison's eyes were closed. My heart ached at the sight, and I swallowed hard, forcing myself to stay composed. Slipping the holster with my sidearm on, I moved to the edge of the bed, my footsteps echoing in the quiet room. Leaning down, I brushed aside her dark hair, the strands silky between my fingers. I pressed a kiss to her temple, lingering for a moment longer than necessary, wishing I could freeze time if only to stay close to her just a little bit longer.

My words were barely a whisper. "Tieni il mio cuore, bellissima."

Hurrying from the apartment, I stepped inside my elevator and leaned against the cool metal walls as it began its descent to the casino. Donny had messaged that they finally found the man responsible for Ana's murder in the basement. Glancing at my watch, I cringed. It was nearly three in the morning, which meant sleep was not anywhere near my future. My mind drifted to the woman waiting in my bed, making my cock twitch. Things were falling into place, including finding my queen.

After stepping off the box, I hurried through the dark halls and keyed the code for the lower level. The heavy, metal door clicked as I pulled it open and stepped into the stairwell. As I descended the steps, muffled cries of terror filled the corridor.

As soon as I stepped into the soundproof room and sealed the door behind me, Donny glanced in my direction. It wasn't the first time all three of us were together in the basement, but it was the first time someone outside the family who wasn't strapped to a chair, was.

"Mr. Cruz Lopez, right hand to Juan Carlos." I joined Donny beside the chair the man was zip-tied to. "Seems you and your boss have been causing some serious problems for my family—and now you've involved an innocent woman."

Spit flew from his lips and landed on my shoe. "Vete a la chingad."

I laughed. "Funny… You're about to learn you're already in hell, and I'm the devil." I backhanded him, causing his head to jerk sideways. "Where. Is. Juan Carlos?"

"He's going to kill you just like that traitor's whore of a sister."

Miguel flew across the room, his fist connecting with Cruz's jaw, sending him sprawling backward. The chair tipped over, crashing to the floor and putting him flat on his back.

The dim light flickered, casting shadows on the grimy walls as I stepped over the downed chair. I pulled out my gun, the weight of it familiar, and pressed it to his knee. "I'll ask again. Where is your boss?"

He sneered, his lips curling into a grotesque grin, blood staining his teeth. Donny and Antonio had already worked him over before I'd arrived, leaving him a battered mess. His eye was swollen shut, and his cheeks were a canvas of bruises, blood, and gashes, courtesy of my brothers' brass knuckles.

The air was thick with tension and the metallic scent of blood. Shifting my weight, I shoved my Glock against his leg and pulled the trigger. The gunshot echoed through the room, a brutal punctuation to his scream. Blood splattered, coating my pants and the floor, the crimson pooling around his trembling body. "This isn't going to be easy, Cruz," I said, my voice cold and unyielding. "You're going to die either way, but you can make it quick by telling us what we want to know."

When he stayed silent, I turned to Miguel. "You want your shot, my friend?" Cruz grunted at my words, making me glance back at his pathetic face. "Surprised, aren't you? See, Cruz." I shifted, stepping away from his body. "When the void happens, and there is a vacuum of power from your Boss's death, the Anastasi's will support the man whose sister you killed. He will take your precious Sureños to a place you never could, and loyalists to your shitty leader, Juna Carlos, will die."

Miguel stood over him. "You thought raping my sister would put us at each other's throats, didn't you?" He slammed the heel of his shoe into Cruz's chest. "But you fucked up by leaving her body at The Sapphire Dagger. You see, Vincenzo doesn't go after women or shoot people in the head. Had you done your research, you'd have known this. For a killer, he has morals." Miguel kicked him again, making Cruz groan beneath his assault. "Don't worry. He's going to show you what he is capable of doing."

I glanced over at my brother—his usual put-together appearance was gone, replaced by a version of him I had prayed we'd never see again. His long hair was loose around his face, a wild mane that mirrored the dangerous glint in his eyes. The suit jacket he usually wore with such precision hung open, revealing a blood-stained shirt underneath. His fists were clenched, knuckles white, and there was a darkness in his expression that sent a chill down my spine.

"You sure about this, Vin?" I asked, my voice low and steady, though my heart pounded in my chest.

Vincent's eyes met mine, a silent storm brewing within them. He gave a slow nod, the hard set of his jaw as he spoke. "Yes. Don't worry; it won't become a problem. But this piece of shit made it personal when he dumped her on my desk like she was nothing more than a whore."

Antonio and I exchanged glances as Vin stepped forward and pulled his blade from his boot. "Do you know who I am?" He leaned down on his knee beside Cruz's face.

Despite the swelling, the man's eyebrows lifted in recognition of who kneeled beside him. "Did she beg for her life like you're going to beg for yours?"

He ran his blade along the piece of shit's cheek, making the once powerful man shrink against the metal and turn into the pathetic waste he'd become on the floor.

I stepped forward and pressed my hand on his shoulder, feeling the tension coiled within him. "You can still change your mind—let one of us do this, Vincenzo."

Vin turned his eyes to me, a flicker of something indefinable passing through them. "Are you asking as my brother or as my Don?"

"Your brother." I glanced around the room, meeting the eyes of our men who stood silently, faces hardened by what they knew was coming. "No one in here will say a fucking word if you get up and walk out."

His jaw tightened, and for a moment, I thought he might relent. But then he shook his head, the darkness in his eyes shifting to something that resembled resolve. "Then don't look at me as your brother… Right now, I need you to be Don Anastasi."

Stepping back, I gave him a single nod and glanced around at the other men in the room. "This is about to get messy."

sixteen

MADISON

IT WAS strange waking up in Massimo's apartment without him, but he never came back after leaving in the middle of the night. I could have laid around, but I had class—and staying locked inside would just give me time to think about the man he'd killed. When I checked my phone, I smiled when I saw that he had at least texted me.

Massimo: Be careful today… I'll be home tonight.

I climbed from bed, wandered into the bathroom and into his closet. My suitcase looked so out of place among his things. Another reminder I didn't fit into this world. Shuffling through my things, I grabbed a pair of leggings and undergarments. Glancing around, I smiled when I spotted a worn T-shirt hanging near the back of the closet. Maybe I was being silly, but I wanted to wear his shirt.

Once I was showered and dressed, I tugged my hair into a ponytail, threw on my Converse, and grabbed my bag. I had to be at class in forty-five minutes, which meant I'd be huffin' it on foot to make it on time. Reading over his message as I slipped into his private elevator, I debated how to reply.

My finger paused over the heart emoji.

Should I send it, or would it send the wrong message? I was pretty sure I was falling for him, but was it love yet?

Even though my heart whispered it was, my head insisted it was still too soon to confess such things. I locked the screen and tucked it away. As I stepped out of the elevator, Freddy, Massimo's driver, called out to me.

"Miss Heart!" he waved, walking toward me. "I have the car around back."

I rubbed my head, confused. "Car?"

"Yes." He took my backpack from me. "Mr. Anastasi has assigned me as your personal driver."

"Personal driver," I repeated like a robot.

Chuckling, he grinned. "You seem surprised."

I should have seen this coming. Massimo's possessiveness was something I would have to grow accustomed to. "You could say that. He didn't mention this to me."

Well, it looks like I'm yours Where to?" He held out an arm, waving me forward.

"The college, I have class." I walked in front of him, wondering how this looked to the other employees. I didn't want them to think I was a gold digger after Massimo's attention. Staying in his apartment and now a personal driver made me look like I was sleeping with him for his money.

"Miss Heart?" Freddy stared at the open door to the SUV. I'd zoned out and was just standing there, staring. "Let's get you there on time, shall we?"

"Oh, sorry."

Freddy set the bag inside and helped me in. Once I was seated, I pulled my phone out. Massimo had to stop with the lavish gifts. I had worked hard to get where I was in life, and I didn't need him to tarnish that by having everyone label me as the girl who sleeps with people to get what she wants.

Me: Massimo, a personal driver, really? We need to talk about this. I don't want people thinking we're together because I want your money.

Massimo: I don't care what they think.

Me: I do!

Massimo: You're the girlfriend of the Don, baby. No one will treat you differently or they will deal with me.

Me: Don't go getting all murderous on me.

Massimo: For your safety and my sanity, use Freddy. We will discuss it more when I return this evening.

Me: Fine…

"Miss Hart, we're here." Looking up, I realized Freddy had pulled to the curb in front of the school's business building.

"Please call me Maddie. If you're going to be carting me around, I'd like to consider us friends. Don't you dare get out and open my door… I'm capable enough to do that on my own."

"Thank you, Miss… I mean, Maddie." Freddy beamed with pride. "What time should I return?"

"I only have two classes today, so I'll be done by two."

"Pick you up here?" He turned in the seat to look at me.

"Yep, here is perfect. See you later, Freddy."

I pushed open the door and grabbed my bag. My phone buzzed in my pocket, so I had to adjust the straps of my backpack on my shoulders to read the text.

Massimo: I miss you.

Those three little words washed away my anger. Smiling like an idiot, I typed out my response.

Me: Really?

Massimo: Yes. I'd much rather be buried inside your tight little pussy.

Me: Jeepers… stop with the dirty talk. I gotta go to class.

Massimo: …

The three dots appeared, causing me to pause at the entrance of my class. They seemed frozen on the screen, making my anxiety spike.

"Miss Heart, are you planning on joining the class or continue standing there staring at your phone?"

My head jerked up. My professor's eyes were drilling through me. "Sorry, I'm coming." I shoved my cell phone into my pocket and rushed inside.

My classes seemed to drag on, and my phone sat tucked silently in my bag—as if mocking me for feeling so needy. When the final class ended, I hurried out of the building, eager to get home. Not hearing from Massimo all day had me on edge.

"Miss Heart," the sound of Freddy's voice caught my attention, and I glanced up.

Tossing my hand up, I'm suddenly bumped from behind. Turning my attention away from my ride, I meet the gaze of a girl who wears an apologetic expression on her face.

"Shit." She smiled as her head shook in embarrassment. "I wasn't watching where I was going."

I smiled, and then everything happened so fast that I had no time to respond.

A single shot echoed in the afternoon air, causing the world to erupt into chaos. The girl I was just about to tell that bumping into me was no big deal dropped to the ground, the concrete beneath her beginning to stain red. Transfixed on the rapidly growing pool of crimson at my feet, I stood unmoving.

I should've been running—everyone else was. Vaguely, I heard my name being called just as another shot sounded. I flinched as my body was slammed into the hard ground.

Blinking through the terror, I realized Freddy was above me, his face pinched in fear…or maybe it was pain, I didn't know. I just knew I couldn't breathe or move.

"Miss Heart." His hands were on me, patting my body as his eyes scanned the area in a panic. "Jesus, girl. Can you hear me?" I blinked. My mind and body were completely disconnected. For a moment, I was an eight-year-old girl locked in a closet again.

A warm hand on my cheek had me drifting back to the present, but I still couldn't form coherent words.

Freddy pushed to his feet and kept his head on a swivel. "I got you, Miss Heart." He lifted my body and in the next moment, we were moving. "Move!" I heard him shout at someone before somehow getting us to the car. "You're gonna be fine, Miss Heart."

But was I really? I didn't know what was real and what wasn't—my brain was stuck playing the sound of the gun and the way that girl looked when she fell to the pavement.

"We're here, Miss Heart." Freddy's voice filtered from the front of the SUV.

My door was jerked open, and Carlisle's familiar eyes scanned my body as he stood at the side of the car. "Jesus Christ, Maddie. What happened?" He brushed my hair from my face. "I got you, sweetheart. Massimo will be here soon."

I was suddenly moving, still clutched against Carlisle's strong chest. Carlisle sat down, cradling me against his side as we sat on the sofa in Massimo's office; I drew my knees to my chest and stared at the wall. When Freddy came in and dropped into the chair behind Massimo's desk, I finally noticed he was hurt.

"Oh God, you're bleeding." I started to get up, but Carlisle grabbed my arm. "Stay, Maddie. Antonio's got Freddy, and I suspect the adrenaline you're feeling is about to crash."

I watched as Antonio entered the room and gave me a tight smile. "Heard you had some excitement today." He removed Freddy's jacket, then his holster. "It's just a graze, Madison; he's going to be fine. Can't say the same for the other guy, though."

I had no idea Freddy was carrying a gun, but it made sense— knowing who he worked for. I closed my eyes as my body began shaking from what I could only assume was shock. I couldn't control my tears or speak. All I could see was that girl's lifeless eyes staring back at mine as they morphed into my mother's dead eyes. There was only one person I needed at that moment.

"I need Massimo."

seventeen

MASSIMO

I SPENT the day cleaning up, literally, the mess left behind by Juan Carlos's henchman. Even my suit had been trashed, a stark reminder that I wasn't a typical nine-to-fiver. I would have instead gone home to shower and clean up, but the thought of Madison seeing me looking like I'd just been on set of *Chainsaw Massacre*, I refrained.

All I wanted to do was go home to my girl. We'd just finished meeting with the police chief, ensuring his fidelity was in line with what we needed. With the dead bodies racking up lately, the last thing I needed was an unhappy cop.

We'd just pulled out of the police station's parking lot when my phone rang. Seeing Carlisle's name had my hackles rising. It was unlike him to call me directly. I pressed the Bluetooth button on the dash, and his voice filled the car.

"Carlisle, what's wrong."

"There's been an incident, sir. Um…you're needed back at the Casino."

Glancing over at Donny, I asked, "Carlisle we're kind of in the middle of something, can't you handle it?"

His silence told me he was trying to find a way to tell me, "Sir, it's Madison." He paused. "There was an issue on campus today, and she had an accident."

"I'll be there in ten."

I hung up, and as soon as I looked at my best friend, he knew without me asking what I needed. "Already on it, Massimo."

The car shot forward. Donny knew me better than my own brothers. He knew from my expression I needed to be where she was.

My fist pounded into the dashboard. "What the fuck? I should have told her to stay home. I knew something like this would happen."

"Calm down." Donny cut his eyes at me, making me growl. "And don't do the pissed-off Don thing with me. I'm not your enforcer right now—I'm your friend. Until we know what happened, you can't blame what's going on with Madison on the Sureños."

"Bullshit." I slammed my fist again. "We just murdered the Sureno's leader, Donny. You know as well as I do that's going to have a blowback."

"Hang on," He threw the car in park. "Calm your ass down before you go in there half-cocked and scare the shit out of her."

"Fuck." I hated that he was right. "What if I'm right, Donny? Because this will surely make her want to leave me." The car barely stopped before I jumped out. Oscar, my guy at the front, opened the door when he saw me coming. I barreled inside, not stopping until I was in my office.

"Massimo." Antonio met my gaze. My eyes trailed over Freddy, "He was shot protecting her. It's just a flesh wound, but your *girl*," he nodded in her direction, "needs you." He was talking, but I wasn't really listening. My eyes were frozen on the woman who owned my heart.

Carlisle stood, his face a mask of worry. He nodded to the couch where Madison was wrapped up in herself, rocking. "She's been asking for you, sir."

"Thank you for taking care of her." I rested my hand on his shoulder as he moved to leave the room. Looking at her fragile state broke my heart. Crouching down in front of her, I brushed her hair back with my hand.

"Madison," I cupped her cheek, "baby, can you hear me?"

Her eyes were glazed over as she stared through me. She was trapped in her own head. I'd seen this before with one of my guys, Alec. He suffered from PTSD from his time spent in the Marines. He told me it was like his brain shut down, blocking out the trigger that set him off.

"Bella," I tried again, this time placing my hand on her leg. She flinched beneath my touch, her eyes swinging down to stare at my hand.

Slowly raising her eyes back to mine, she blinked.

"Massimo?"

"Yeah, bella. It's me."

She leaped into my arms, nearly knocking me onto my ass. Her arms and legs wrapped around me, clinging to my body in a vise grip. I rubbed her back as I rocked her.

"It's okay. I got you."

"Massimo," she whimpered my name. "That girl…she's… she's…"

"I know. It's going to be all right, Madison. I'm here now. You're safe." She hiccupped, a sob breaking free as I held her in my arms. Glancing back at my brother and Freddy, "Thank you, Freddy. What you did today–well, I can't ever repay you."

"A flesh wound is nothing. I'd give my life for her, sir. She's special." He stood and made his way out of the office, leaving just me and Antonio alone with Madison.

"I know." I clutched her body to mine. "It's looking like someone from the Sureños is pissed about the change in leadership."

"And the man who took a shot at her?" I grunted.

"Dead. Freddy got a shot off. He really went above his duty tonight." Antonio grumbled, his lips pinched in frustration. "Someone tried to kill her today, Massimo. They're not going to stop until they get revenge. Miguel is on his way, and he's pissed. Someone in his ranks is trying to usurp his position."

"She can't stay here." I pressed a kiss to her head. "Let me get her upstairs. Call Vin. I need him to handle things when Miguel gets here, and I need you to meet me upstairs in an hour. We need a plan an end this bullshit and keep her safe."

Her head lolled against me, and I was sure her mind was still trapped in its safe haven. I hated that my darkness had touched her like this—that she was threatened because of my business. Whoever did this was going to pay…with their life.

"We'll protect her, fratello." Antonio pressed his hand to my shoulder and leaned down to press a kiss to Madison's forehead. "She's good for you, Massimo."

"Massimo." Her soft voice washed over me, easing something inside my chest.

"I got you, bella. You're safe." I kissed her cheek.

"I want to go home." She started crying again. "Please, Massimo. I don't want to be here."

"Home?" My gut churned as I glanced at my brother, who was still watching.

This was it.

This was the moment she *left* me.

"Yes, take me upstairs, please. I can't be down here right now." She cried harder, gripping my shirt in her fists.

I blinked, stunned at her words. "You want to go to my apartment?"

"Yes, home. Please," she mumbled against my shirt, her tears soaking the material.

Antonio smirked and gave his nod of approval as he moved out of my way. "See you in an hour."

Drew, one of the guards, stood like a sentinel outside the

hallway to my office. "Sir." He gave me a sympathetic nod, his eyes glancing at Madison.

"I'm taking Madison home. Please let them know I'll have my phone. And Drew…" I paused. "Tell *everyone*… Touch what is mine, and I'll set the world ablaze. Some lines, once crossed, leave nothing but ashes and regret."

"Yes, sir."

He followed me to the elevators and ensured we got on without anyone stopping us. Madison never budged, clinging to me as if her life depended on it. Once inside the apartment, I carried her straight to the bathroom and set her down on the bench.

She sat stone-still as I moved around the room. I turned the water on, dumped in some bath oils, and dimmed the lights. Taking care of her was my number one priority, right? The world outside could go fuck itself.

"Baby." I lifted her chin. Her face was swollen and red from crying. Tears still fell helplessly, staining her cheeks further. "I've started a bath. Let's clean you off."

Her leggings were torn at her knees, the skin beneath them ripped and covered in gravel and blood. I wanted to be pissed no one had noticed, but she didn't need my anger right now. "I'm only going to grab some towels and bath stuff."

Her eyes tracked me as I moved around the room, gathering stuff. She watched as I turned the water on and filled the tub. I squatted in front of her and brushed her hair back from her face. Her beautiful face was swollen from the tears she'd been crying.

"I'm going to undress you now, okay?" I ran my hand down her arm. "Madison, do you understand?" She nodded as I pulled her to her feet. "You good? "My hands hovered at her waist, and her eyes searched mine. "Still with me?"

She nodded once, holding my gaze. "I'm going to take this off." I gripped the edge of her pants and slowly eased them over her legs. Her panties were next, leaving her bare from the waist down. When my fingers went to her shirt, I couldn't help but smile. She was wearing one of my workout shirts. I growled when I noticed the blood at the hem. After quickly removing the fabric, I tossed it in the trash. There was a good chance the blood belonged to the girl who'd unknowingly taken the bullet for her.

Next, I slipped my fingers beneath her bra and released the snap against her back. "Almost done." I discarded the lace on the floor and moved my hands back to her hips. "God, you're beautiful." She looked me over. "Let's get you in the tub, yeah?"

eighteen

MASSIMO

MADISON'S FINGERS laced with mine as I helped her into the warm water and watched as she sank until she was sitting. "Take your time, bella." I strode to the door.

"Wait," she called out, halting my movement. "Don't leave me." Madison's eyes pleaded. She was too afraid to be alone—maybe because of what happened earlier.

"You want me to stay?" I tilted my head, waiting for her answer, praying I had heard right.

"Please."

One word held so much meaning, and I understood. I kicked off my shoes, then slowly stripped off each article of clothing. Her eyes never left my body as I slowly worked the buttons of my shirt and tossed it to the floor in a heap. My pants came next. I released the snap, eased the zipper down, then shoved them down my legs, taking my boxers with them. Like a lion, I stalked toward Madison, my eyes never breaking contact.

"Slide forward."

Madison scooted up, giving me room to crawl in behind her. My legs stretched out beside hers, cradling her between my thighs. Once I was seated fully, I snaked my arms around her midsection and pulled her against my front. Leaning back, Madison rested her head on my chest.

"I was nine when my mother died." I stiffened beneath Madison when her words came out in a whisper. "We were home alone because my dad was still at work. I remember we were playing a board game in my room when we heard the crash. My mother stood up and ushered me into my closet to hide. We lived in one of those houses that had doors with slats on the closets. You know the kind I'm talking about?" She paused, seemingly to gather her wits, then continued. "She put me inside and told me not to make any noises, no matter what I saw or heard. I didn't understand what was happening. I was just a kid. My mom covered me with a blanket, then kissed me before she shut the doors and went to call the police. I didn't understand why she didn't hide with me. If she had, maybe she'd still be alive."

I squeezed her leg, brushing her skin beneath the water. I covered her hand with mine, lacing our fingers together, needing the connection to ground the rage I was feeling as she continued. "I watched as she picked up the phone to call 9-1-1, but two men came into the room. I couldn't see their faces, but I could hear them. They demanded to know if there was anyone else there with her. I heard her tell them she was alone, and that we had nothing for them. She begged them to leave…to spare her. One of the men slapped her, then…"

Her body tensed as if she were replaying the memory in her mind. "He pointed his gun at her head and pulled the trigger. I shoved the blanket into my mouth, stifling the scream that was trying to escape my body. They ransacked the dresser, getting a few hundred dollars in jewelry before sirens sounded in the distance. I remember the blood and the way her eyes stared at me from the floor. I stayed in the corner of the closet for what felt like hours, just holding the gaze of my dead mother. My father got home as the police arrived which was only moments later. His screams haunted me for months. It wasn't until he regained his senses that he looked for me.

"Funny thing is, you'd think a child would only live through one tragedy in their life, and maybe that's true for most, but I wasn't that fortunate. My dad fell into a deep depression and started drinking. One minute, he was the only thing I had left, and then, just like that, he was gone. He killed himself and a family when he drove home drunk one night. By ten years old, I'd buried my mother and my father."

"I'm so sorry, baby." My fingers brushed the wet tendrils of her hair from her shoulder.

"Massimo." She shifted in the tub and straddled me in the water. "I'm nobody. I grew up in the system and bounced from home to home. It wasn't until my senior year that I realized I could control my fate. I got into college and finally saw something good in my life. You deserve someone who matches your worth."

Cupping her face in my hands, "Fuck, look at me, bella. From the moment I saw you, I knew you were the one for me. Your worth is more than you realize. In fact, it's me who's not worthy of you. My heart was black before you. Madison, you're the air I breathe. I've fallen in love with you."

I pressed a quick kiss to her lips. "I know it's probably too fast for you, but know this… I'll wait a lifetime for you to feel the same. Until then, let me guard your heart and be your shield in this world."

I brushed my thumb across her cheek, swiping a lone tear that had escaped. I hoped she could see it in my eyes that I would burn the world down to protect her at any cost–and while that feeling should scare me, it didn't.

"You love me?" Madison whispered, her hands gripping his shoulders.

"So much it scares me." I rested my forehead on hers as I wrapped my arms and held her against me. My eyes found hers. "If you ever walked away, I'd cease to exist. "

Her breasts pressed against my chest, her hard nipples poking into my skin. I moved, causing her center to rub against my already hardening cock.

"Madison." I groaned. "As much as I love holding you like this…you need to stop moving, or I won't be able to control myself."

Madison adjusted her legs wider, bending them so her knees were pressed to the porcelain basin beside my hips. "I need to forget tonight. Give me a better memory." Pressing her lips to mine, her hands trailed down my chest.

"You've had a traumatic event. You need time to recover." I grunted when her fingers wrapped around my dick. "Fuck, Madison. Oh, hell…" I hissed through my teeth as she slowly sank down onto my erection. Madison held my stare as she slowly moved against my shaft. I gripped her hips, holding her in place. "Are you sure this is what you want?"

"Please." Madison bit her bottom lip as she rocked her body, forcing my cock to move inside her.

Losing control, I leaned forward and captured her nipple in my mouth. I suckled the tiny pink bud between my lips, drawing out the most sinful moan from her while her hair fell around us as she rode my cock. My hands held her steady, stilling her movements. I had other plans.

"Wait," I commanded. "Hold on to me."

I pressed my hands over the edge of the tub and pushed our bodies up, causing my erection to slip out of her body. Madison's legs wrapped around my waist, holding her slick skin against mine as I lifted us out of the water. Moving to the bench beside the tub, I laid her on her back. Her body slid against the leather, soaking the floor beneath us as the water dripped from our skin.

Positioning myself on top of her, my fingers dug into the rectangular seat, holding on as I plowed back into her tight channel. Madison's nails bit into my neck as her legs wound around my back. I drove in and out of her, frantic to fill her tight pussy. Her walls pulsed around my shaft, demanding my release as I continued to pound into her. The bench moved beneath us, the wooden legs scraping across the floor as we ravaged each other.

Madison's grip tightened to the point of pain as she cried out my name, and her orgasm burst from her. Her slick juices coated my dick, the sound of how wet she was filled the bathroom. It was the trigger to my release, making my dick swell even more before erupting and coating her walls with my seed. My thrusts eased as her legs untangled from my back and planted on the floor.

"Are you okay?" I pressed a kiss to her neck before standing. My cock slipped out from between her legs, dripping the evidence of our union on the bench. I helped her stand and then led us into the enclosure and turned on the showerheads. Hot water washed over us as we rinsed the evidence of our furious lovemaking down the drain. The alpha inside me hated she was washing away my scent, but there would be plenty of time to mark her again and again. I laced my fingers with Madison's and guided her from the shower. I wrapped her in a towel and led us out of the bathroom and toward the bed.

She watched as I moved effortlessly around the room, then disappeared into the bathroom. When I emerged, her eyes were still trained on the doorway as if she was waiting for me to emerge. I held up the clothes I had fisted in my hand. "Let's get you dressed. Antonio will be here in a few moments, and I'd rather he not see you naked."

Madison had barely pulled a pale blue linen dress over her head when the elevator opened, revealing both of my brothers. Vincenzo had an air of violence around him, one I was sure had to do with our earlier meeting. Antonio wore his typical smirk—the one I wanted to slap off on more than one occasion. Madison stood in front of me as we took our seats in the living room.

"Hey Maddiemoo." Antonio greeted her with his killer smile, making me growl in irritation. The sound made Antonio smirk even broader as he sat down opposite Madison and me. "How are you?"

"I mean, someone shot a girl today, but otherwise." Madison shrugged. She joked with my brother so effortlessly that I wanted to choke him—and he had a fucking nickname for her?

"Cut it with the cutesy nicknames, Antonio." I tugged her into my lap. "What have you learned?"

"Boss… This was personal. Miguel might be gaining control of the Sureños now that Juan has gone to ground, but the organization is massive. It's going to take time to weed out those loyal to Juan." He sighed. "That being said… I'm pretty sure the hit was intended for Madison."

Madison stiffened against my legs. "What do you mean it was meant for me?" Her voice came out as a whisper.

My hand smoothed down her hair as I cupped her cheek, turning her to look at me. "I've angered some powerful people, bella. We think—no, we know, they're trying to make a play against my family."

"But—" I covered her lip with my thumb and shook my head.

"This isn't about you. It's about me. I'm so sorry I've put you in danger, bella." I lifted her chin. "I will do everything to keep you safe."

"We all will," Antonio spoke, making her jerk her head from my hold and look at him. "Which is why I think she should disappear for a little while."

"What?" Madison and I spoke at the same time.

"If she isn't here, you can focus," Vincenzo finally said. "You've been distracted, Massimo. Rightfully so, but you know as well as I do they'll use her to get to you. Juan Carlos might be in hiding, but someone is still following his orders. Miguel is doing everything he can to flush the traitors out, but until then—she's in danger."

I glanced between my brother and the woman I loved, realization smacking me in the face. The easiest way to destroy a kingdom was to destroy the heart of one. In this case, the heart was the women we loved.

My eyes found Madison watching with a confused but worried gaze. Her brows were knitted together while her eyes darted back and forth as if trying to piece together the situation. I had no choice… She wasn't safe—I couldn't risk her being hurt again. And they wouldn't stop until she was dead.

"Bella." She held my stare. "Put on your shoes; you're leaving."

nineteen

MADISON

"PUT ON YOUR SHOES; you're leaving."

His words were like a bullet–striking me straight to the heart. "I'm sorry, what?" I blinked, sure I'd heard him wrong.

"You need to leave." He moved across the room, gone was the man who'd spent the last hour showing me love; in his place, the man I feared. Hurrying behind him, I grabbed my Converse and started haphazardly putting them on.

Antonio moved toward me. "Being the girlfriend of someone in the mafia, much less the head of the mafia means you'll always be in danger to some extent."

His words hit me like a ton of bricks. He was right. Massimo's life was full of uncertainty and danger. I didn't know if I could live like that forever. "This is a mistake. I can't live like this."

Massimo stopped and looked at me, his eyes glazed over with regret. "A mistake? What you feel for me is a mistake?"

"No, but…" I swallowed. "I don't want a life where I'm always afraid."

He walked across the room and stood in front of me, and he cupped my chin in his hand. "It won't always be this way, bella."

"Can you promise me that? I've lived my whole life in fear to some extent. Always looking over my shoulder, wondering if I'd end up like my parents. I don't want that life, Massimo."

"Please let me get you to safety. When this is all over, if you still want your freedom, I'll let you go. But I can't do that right now—not knowing you'd be in danger." I could tell even uttering the words gave him pain.

Offering me my freedom to ensure my happiness meant he really loved me, and as much as I didn't think I wanted this life, I wasn't sure I could walk away from him.

"Okay," I whispered just before he pressed his lips to mine.

His kiss was hungry and full of need. When he broke away, he rested his forehead against mine.

"I love you, Madison. I'll do anything to make you happy, even if that means walking away from you." He turned and stared at his brother. "Let's go."

"Wait… Where are you sending me?"

Antonio smiled. "With me."

Massimo growled. "You're going to Italy. My brother has to return there to take care of some business. It's the perfect time to get you out of here and safe—while I end this fucking mess." He turned. "I won't let anything happen to you. I meant what I said earlier, Madison. You're the air I breathe and the light in my soul. I've fallen in love with you, and no one, not even a sad pussy like Juan Carlos, will take you away from me."

"I don't want to go, but I understand."

"I don't want you to either, but it's the only way I'll know you're safe. If you stay here, you'll be a distraction. I can't keep you safe and do my job. Please, I need you somewhere. Whoever is doing this can't touch you, and no one would dare make such an attempt in Sicily. Not with my father watching over you."

"Why is this happening?" Tears spilled down my face as we gathered in the elevator.

"Killing the head of the Sureños pissed someone off within the organization."

My naivety was showing, but I still didn't understand why this meant I had to go running for the hills. "What does that have to do with me?"

"He wants to hit me where it hurts. My guess is Juan has figured out your importance to me. Taking you out would give him the chance he needs to bring me to my knees." Massimo caressed my cheek. He laced his fingers with mine as we stepped out of the elevator and headed toward the exit. "You're mine now. Nothing is more important to me than you. Please do this for me." He gripped my hand tighter as we stepped out into the Vegas night air. "I love you enough to walk away from you when this is all over. If you can't handle the life loving me would entail, I'll set your heart free when I know you're no longer in danger."

"I can't think about this right now. You know how I feel about violence, and everything about you screams mayhem. I'll go for now. I need time to think." I gave him a half-hearted smile. "But what about you? Will you be safe?"

Massimo held my face in his hands as he gazed into my eyes. "Don't worry about me, bella. I will burn this city down to get what I want." He covered my lips with his own. "I'll come for you when it's over. I have to go." Kissing me one last time, Massimo eased open the car door of the awaiting SUV.

I never thought my life could get any more messed up than it already was. I was wrong. Staring out the tiny window of Massimo's private jet, my mind drifted back over the last twenty-four hours.

A woman was dead—a hit meant for me as a message to Massimo. Glancing up, I found Antonio's eyes watching me. "We should land in Paris in about forty-five minutes."

"Paris?" I held his gaze. "I thought we were going to Italy?"

He snorted. "We are, but we have to stop to refuel. We'll only be on the ground long enough to do that."

"Oh." I shrugged, turning back to look out the window. It was then I noticed the lights below us, indicating civilization.

"You slept through the first refueling. Are you hungry?" Antonio pushed up from the seat across me.

"We landed before?" I rubbed my head, shocked I'd slept through anything

"Yes." Antonio reached across the seat and pressed his hand to my leg. "You should really try to eat."

"I'm not hungry."

His lips pressed into a thin, tight line, and his nose wrinkled slightly in irritation as he nodded. "That's fine for now. When we get to Sicily, I'll expect you to eat then. I'll be back. I need to speak with the pilot. The restroom is back there." He pointed to the back of the plane. "Go freshen up. It'll make you feel better." He walked toward the cockpit and disappeared behind the door.

Pushing myself up to stand, I gripped the back of the seat and steadied myself. I made my way to the rear of the plane before locking myself inside the lavatory. I expected it to be smaller, but knowing Massimo, it wasn't a surprise to see he made sure it was comfortable.

The room had a standup shower, toilet, and vanity. Pressing my hands against the edge of the porcelain counter, I cringed at my reflection. My hair looked as though it hadn't been brushed in days, and my face…well, it was swollen and red. Turning the water on cold, I then dipped my hands beneath the stream, filling my palms, then pressed the cool liquid against my skin. I snagged a hand towel off the wall and wiped it across my wet skin until it was dry. My eyes looked tired and weary, making the reflection staring back at me in the mirror a stranger. I quickly used the bathroom, washed my hands one more time, then turned off the faucet.

Making my way back to my seat, I took a deep breath, and sat down. Antonio was watching me as I slipped back into my seat. He reached across me and snapped my belt into place before I had the chance to do it myself.

"What will happen when we get to Italy?"

"A driver will be waiting when we land. Massimo briefed our father on the situation before we left Vegas."

"Why were you going there in the first place?"

Antonio glanced out the window. "My grandfather is dying." He took a breath and looked back over at me, his eyes filled with so much sadness I regretted even asking. "I've always been the odd man out of my three brothers. I'm not really their equal, but grandfather has always made me feel—I dunno, important. I guess you got stuck with the fucked-up brother. Sorry, Maddiemoo."

"Great, so two fricked-up people will rely on one another." I snorted. "But I'm glad it's you, Antonio. Your other brother is scary."

He laughed. "You're not fucked up. And yeah. Vin is scary as shit."

"Really, Antonio? I've fallen in love with your brother, a mobster. I saw him shoot a man in the head…and then an innocent girl took a bullet meant for me. All because of whatever your family is involved in. I should tuck my tail and run, but I can't. Not yet. How is that not messed up?"

"You said not yet. Does that mean you might still leave him?"

I turned my head away from him, glancing out at the moving scenery as the plane descended.

"I don't know. Please don't tell him. I don't need him worrying about me when his life is in danger."

"Madison." He took my hand in his. "Massimo is a good

man. We might be mobsters in your eyes, but to me…" He sighed. "We're a family who takes care of those we love."

"These feelings he says he has could fade, then what? I'll be left broken-hearted. I just need to clear my head and think. That's the only reason I agreed to come here."

The pilot came over the intercom, announcing our descent into Paris. We would only be on the ground long enough to refuel, leaving little time to appreciate the scenery just outside my window.

"It's beautiful, isn't it?" Antonio smiled as he watched the lights pass by while we landed.

"I never thought the first time I saw the Eiffel Tower I'd be on the run."

"Massimo will bring you back to enjoy what Paris has to offer."

"It doesn't matter. It will forever hold the tarnish of this moment." I pressed my head against my seat as the plane bounced across the ground. "I just want to sleep. Maybe this is all a bad dream, and I'll wake up to everything being normal again."

twenty

MASSIMO

TWO WEEKS... Two fucking weeks without Madison, and I was no closer to finding the fucker who was hiding Juan Carlos. Miguel was restless as well. The men of the Sureños were clearly divided. Some took to showing him loyalty immediately. Others had found what being in limbo cost them.

"The cops were here sniffing around, demanding to speak with Madison," Donny grunted as we sat around discussing the events. "They are still digging into the shooting at the college and are suspicious why she left the country."

"Alec, I'll need you to pull some footage of our illustrious D.A. It's time I put some pressure on him to make this go away. Donny," I turned toward him, "where are we on flushing out who is behind this?"

"I got a few guys on the ground."

The door opened, and my brother, Vin, walked in. "Fratello."

He pressed his hand to my shoulder and took the seat beside me. "How's Madison?"

"Antonio said he had to give her something to help her sleep. He said she is struggling with," I swallowed, "everything."

"Is this girl worth the trouble?" He slid into the chair across from me. "You killed an assistant district attorney over her."

"This girl," I grated out through a clenched jaw, "is worth setting the whole damn planet on fire."

"Calm down, brother." Vincenzo put his hand up defensively. "I only needed confirmation of what I already suspected."

"And what did you suspect?"

"That you found your soulmate. Grandmother has told us since we were young that we'd know when we found her. Now, what are we going to do to show these motherfuckers the Anastasis aren't to be trifled with?"

I gritted my teeth. "It was bad enough that the motherfucker stole from us but taking a hit out on Madison—whoever it is royally fucked up coming after me."

"He came after all of us, Massimo. If Madison is as important to you as you say, she's family now. No one goes after our family and lives." I nodded, his words only fueling my rage.

"Have Alec find me everything on Juan Carlos. I want to know who his family is, his whores, his brothers, everything. Donny put together the best guys. I want them to dig until they find who is still covering for this motherfucker. Have Miguel put some guys on it, too… if we can find one, we'll find him. Remind Miguel If he wants this alliance as bad as he says he does—he's going to have to prove it."

My phone vibrated against my thigh. Slipping the device from my pocket, I saw Antonio's face fill my screen. "Antonio." I pressed the speaker, setting the phone on the table. "You're on speaker. How is everyone—any problems?"

"Don't worry, my beautiful cargo is safe."

"Hands off, little brother," I growled, eliciting a laugh from Vincenzo. "You may be blood, but I will cut off your dick if you even think of touching her. Is she near you?" I tapped my fingers on the table. "Put her on the phone."

"Hang on." I could hear Antonio's muffled voice as he spoke to someone in the background. "Sorry, brother, she still doesn't want to talk to you."

"Fuck…" I slammed my hand down on the table.

Vincenzo gripped my arm. "Give her time."

"Listen to Vin, Massimo. Madison still seems pretty rattled. Plus, she's here, miles away from home, with *our* parents. Her life is completely turned upside down, not to mention she's seen two people gunned down—one by the man she's in love with. That takes time coming to terms with."

"Fine. Antonio, take care of her. Tell her this will all be over soon, and I'll come for her." Donny stormed back in as I was setting my phone down. "That was fast."

"You can thank Miguel. We have someone downstairs."

My feet carried me swiftly through the casino down to the basement. Vincenzo whispered something to Donny and headed in the opposite direction. "He's going to get some leverage. He'll be back."

You'd never know the number of people who'd lost their lives protecting the wrong man. This mother fucker was no different. In fact, I suspected he would break when he learned just how much leverage I had on him.

Stepping forward, I gripped the handle of the gun in my palm and pressed the barrel against his temple. "Where is Juan Carlos?"

The vile creature had the balls to smirk. He *fucking* smirked. Like this was some kind of game. Well, he could deny it all he wanted, but the tattooed thirteen beneath his eye told a different tale—the classic mark of the Mexican mafia, the Sureños—not to mention the blue bandanna wrapped around his head. And based on what Miguel told Donny, this was Juan's second.

"You are a dumb motherfucker." Donny shook his head and leaned against the metal table. "He makes Juan Carlos look like child's play, and being his second, I'm sure you've seen your boss do plenty of scary shit." There was a brief flicker of understanding before his mask of denial fell back in place.

"Do. Not. Fuck. With. Me." I pressed the metal harder into his skull. "I have no problem splattering your brains across the cement."

"Come on, cholo." Donny stood and moved to stand beside me, slipping his blade out in the process. He pressed his hand into the scum's shoulder as he dug a knife into his side. "You're going to die, anyway."

"I know nothing."

"How about your family?" I clenched my jaw, moving away to give the others room to torture. I wasn't going to get my hands dirty this time. I was leaving that to Donny. I'd ruined enough suits for this trash. "Does your wife or daughter know Juan?"

He groaned his words, his face pinched in concern. "Leave my family alone."

"If I can't get what I want from you, I'll get it from them. I will stop at nothing to find Juan Carlos."

He stuttered out his words in broken English, but the message was clear. "There will be a thousand more like me to protect him."

I smiled, knowing he was slowly crumbling. When a man's family was threatened, those carefully constructed walls tended to fall. "We're getting somewhere, Donny. He finally admitted to knowing Juan."

"Maybe cutting off his fingers will break him." Donny moved toward the table and grabbed a cutting tool from the surface. "What do you say, Enrico? Fingers?" I watched as Donny pulled his bound hands toward him and nestled his pointer finger between the metal blades.

"Fuck you." Enrico pressed his lips together, holding my stare.

"You heard him, Donny, he said finger."

Donny gripped the cable cutters, forcing them closed around his digit. Blood spurted out, spraying crimson droplets across

Donny's shirt. Enrico screamed as the metal blades of the tool bit into his flesh, snapping the bone clean. The finger dropped to the floor as blood oozed out across the cement.

"I'll ask you again." I grabbed his hair, yanking his head back. "Where is Juan?"

"I can't tell you," he moaned.

"Drew," I called out to one of my guys leaning against the wall. "Get Vincenzo."

"What?" His eyes widened. "No…" The funny part was I wished Vincenzo was coming in for the reason this bastard thought.

He gasped when Drew came back through the door with my brother. Vincenzo was dragging Enrico's wife beside him. She was crying and fighting against Vincenzo's hold.

"I told you I'd do anything. Now, tell me where I can find Juan, or the next finger that comes off will be hers."

Vincenzo shoved her into a chair across from him and strapped her ankles down with zip ties. The plastic bit into her flesh, splitting the skin open. He held her arm in his, stretching her fingers out in front of him. Donny moved in front of them and wrapped the cigar cutter around her finger.

"Enrico," she sobbed. "Please, don't do this. I know nothing."

"Last chance, Enrico. Where. Is. Juan. Carlos?"

He stayed still, refusing to speak and forcing my hand. I hated to inflict violence on women, but I was desperate. Juan had fucked with my family in more ways than one, and I needed to find and kill him.

"Donny." I nodded toward her hand, and Enrico's wife screamed out as he snipped off her finger, causing her husband to yell out as his wife's cries filled the room.

"Stop! Please! No more. I'm so sorry, baby." Her sobs echoed off the walls as she pleaded for her life. "I'll tell you, but please leave her alone."

He began giving us the information we sought, including places Juan frequented and what times. Once he'd provided what we needed, I glanced at Donny.

"Enrico, know your daughter will be taken care of. She'll be taken to a good foster home."

"What? Please… I told you everything you asked for."

Donny pulled out his gun and pressed it to Enrico's wife's head. "Your boss shouldn't have fucked with us, Enrico. You're a means to an end, I'm afraid."

The muffled sound of Donny's bullet caused Enrico to jump. He cried out as his wife's brain splattered across the cement wall behind them. Her lifeless body slumped to the floor, the chair tipping over with her. Her vacant eyes stared at him, mocking his poor decision. He cried out, turning his head toward me to scream obscenities, seconds before the final bullet took his life.

"Take their bodies and dump them on Juan's doorstep. I want him to know I'm coming for him. I'll be upstairs. I need to make a phone call."

I walked out of the room and leaned against the closed door. Even though this was a common part of overseeing the family business, it didn't get any easier. Taking a life was hard, no matter who you were.

Drew eyed me as I started toward the stairs. "Still haven't talked to Madison?"

"No." I paused, "Antonio assures me he's been taking care of her, but I won't believe it until I hear it from her own lips."

"I'm sure Antonio has it under control."

Dusting my hands down my pants, I took a deep breath. It had been two weeks since I'd sent Madison to my parents in Italy, and she still wouldn't take my calls. Antonio assured me she was getting better, but I needed to hear her voice to know for myself.

"That's what I'm afraid of," I grunted my unease as I started my ascent to the casino.

twenty-one

MADISON

"I STILL CAN'T BELIEVE this is your family's place?" I smiled as we pulled into the circular drive.

"Yeah. It has been the Anastasis' abode for generations. My grandmother and grandfather were married here, as were my parents. I suppose when it's our time…" I noticed Antonio's eyes lose their focus for a moment as his voice trailed off. "We will all marry here as well."

The last two weeks hadn't been so bad. Antonio had shown me places in Italy that were unimaginable. He even promised me a trip to Venice. Carmela and Celestina, the twins, had also spent time with me. I'd learned that they were nearly done with design school and planned on joining Massimo and his brothers in Vegas. They wanted to open their own clothing shop, selling their designs. Celestina asked me to work for them when they got there. Since I would have a business degree, they felt I would be an asset to their master plan.

"Antonio!" Massimo's mother pushed out of her chair and said, "Come get some food and sit."

"I'm not hungry." I blushed, looking down at my feet.

"Bella," Antonio growled with a tone filled with warning. "You should just talk to him."

"Antonio," his mother scolded.

"No, Mother. I promised Massimo I'd look after her. She hasn't eaten a decent meal in days. Yeah, Maddie, I've seen you pretending to finish your meal. If I hadn't threatened to cut off Peter's cock, he would have kept covering for you."

"Antonio. Jesus." I groaned, covering my face.

"Madison." His mother gasped, turning to grab my hand. "Let's get you some food. You must stay well for Massimo."

"Thank you, Mrs. Anastasi, I'll try."

"Please, dear… I told you to call me Gio. We're going to be family one day."

I glanced at Antonio, who shrugged. I followed them inside, gave in to their watchful stares, and managed to get the majority of my meal down. When we were done, Antonio led me into the massive media room and sat down.

"Let's watch a movie. Because I know you don't want to talk about my brother, though I think you need to stop fighting yourself and call him."

I stuck out my tongue and plopped down on the leather couch beside him. Glancing at the clock, I yawned. "I'll watch some of it—I'm pooped from today." My body had finally adjusted to the time difference, but Antonio and I had spent the day exploring parts of Sicily. We even went swimming at one of the local beaches. He was doing his best to keep my mind off Massimo and his mind of his grandfather's impending death. The doctors hadn't given him much longer, and while everyone was doing their best to hide their sadness, I could see it clear as day in his eyes.

When I saw his head roll to the side, I snickered. He was worn out, too. "Are you even watching this movie?"

During our time together, Antonio and I had become close. He confided in me things only his grandfather knew, making me fall in love with him—*like* a brother. I shared my past with him and even my feelings for Massimo. He knew I was struggling to accept that love could happen so quickly and that I was terrified of what loving him would mean. Seeing him try to ignore me, I dug my foot into him harder, making him burst out in laughter.

"Oh no, you don't." He lurched toward me, pinning me under the weight of his body. His fingers dug into my sides, causing me to writhe beneath him. I couldn't control the laughter.

"Stop! Oh my God, Antonio… You're going to make me pee myself."

The sudden vibration against my leg had us both pausing. "I'll get it." I fished in his pocket and pulled out his phone, inadvertently answering the FaceTime call in the process.

"What. The. Fuck?" Massimo's voice bellowed through the screen.

"Massimo." Antonio bolted upright, grabbing the phone and shoving me off him. "It's not what it looks like."

The screen went dead, leaving Antonio and me staring at his phone. "Shit, he has the wrong idea. Give me the phone. I'll talk to him." He snatched the phone and pressed his contact, but it went directly to voicemail. "Fuck, he's not answering."

"How could he think—" My breath caught in my chest. "You're his brother, for God's sake."

Antonio stood and palmed the back of his head. "I'm the flirty brother, Madison. They think I'm a womanizer and you're beautiful. I'd never do that to him—but he isn't thinking straight. And you aren't talking to him and then happened to be straddling me when he called. What would you think, sweetheart?"

"Give me the phone, Antonio." I held my hand out. "It will be okay. I'll take care of this."

Standing, I walked to the window as the sound of ringing filled my ear. Massimo's voicemail picked up again, forcing me to leave a message. "Massimo, it's me. It's not what you think. Please call me back. I miss you." Disconnecting the call, I handed Antonio the phone. "He'll call back. I know he will." I folded my arms across my chest.

"You don't know my brother like I do. This is bad. I need to call my brother…and then my father about what happened. Massimo is going to be on a warpath. Excuse me." Antonio left the room, leaving me alone with my thoughts.

I scurried over to the desk where the phone Antonio got me when we arrived, sat charging. I'd avoided talking to

Massimo since arriving in Italy, needing time to sort through my feelings. After hearing the hurt in his voice, I knew without a doubt that I was in love with him. My heart ached, and I needed to clear up this misconception. Pressing the phone to my ear, I waited, hoping he'd answer me, but it went to voicemail again.

"Please, Massimo. You need to let me explain. I know it looked bad, but it's not like that with Antonio. He's like my brother. We've gotten close. Don't be mad at me. Answer the phone…please. I want to tell you how I feel, but not like this. I love you…I do. I'm sorry I've ignored you. I just needed some time. Massimo." I sighed. "Please call me."

I texted him, pleading for him to pick up his phone. If I'd seen him like that with another woman, I'd be livid, so I understood his reaction to some extent, but this was his brother.

Who could he think I—no, we'd—betray him like that?

Sliding the phone into my pocket, I headed to my room. It was closing in on midnight, and I had to write a paper for school. Somehow, Massimo had convinced the college to allow a final project submission instead of attending any more classes. His status in Vegas seemed to pay off in more ways than I could comprehend. Antonio stood in the kitchen speaking with his father, Giacomo, when I made my way to the stairs. Giacomo glanced my way, a sympathetic expression on his face.

"Everything will be all right, ragazza dolce." I forced a smile back. He'd taken to calling me sweet girl in Italian since arriving.

"Thank you, sir." But deep down, I wondered if he was wrong.

Had I just screwed up the best thing in my life because I was being stubborn? I shut myself inside my room and began stripping off my clothes. I tugged on Massimo's shirt, which I'd worn to bed every night since arriving. It was the only thing I had of him here in Italy. Antonio had taken me shopping the day after I arrived. That man had more fashion sense than any woman I'd ever met.

I glanced at my screen, wishing for a response to appear. He needed to know it wasn't what he thought. Antonio would never cross that line, not only because he didn't see me like that but his loyalty to his family was more important. With his grandfather dying, Antonio felt as though he had no one to lean on until me. He was the brother I'd never had. I just needed Massimo to see that.

By the time I finally closed my eyes, I'd sent nearly a dozen text messages and left almost as many messages. Curling up on myself, I let the tears fall. It wasn't supposed to end like this, yet that's how I was feeling.

Like our time was over before it had even begun.

Clasping the phone against my chest, I let sleep take claim to me. Morning would come sooner than I wanted, and I feared I would find myself broken-hearted and confused soon enough.

twenty-two

MASSIMO

PISSED OFF, I threw the phone across my desk and watched as it bounced off the wooden surface and scattered to the floor at Donny's feet. The sight of it lying there, lifeless and mocking, only added to my growing frustration.

"Everything all right, boss?" Donny asked, closing the door behind him.

"No. Everything is not fucking all right. Tell me you've found Juan Carlos."

Donny bent over and picked up my phone. He glanced at the screen, then at me, raising a brow in question. "You have thirty missed calls."

"I am aware of how many calls I've missed." I snapped, the edge in my voice sharper than intended.

Donny thumbed the screen. "And at least a dozen text messages from Madison. What's going on, Massimo?"

Hearing my first name from Donny's lips was a rare occurrence, signaling he was in friend mode, not muscle. I sighed and ran my fingers through my hair, trying to collect my thoughts.

"I called her earlier."

"Okay, and?"

"It was almost eleven p.m. her time," I continued, the anger bubbling just beneath the surface.

He shuffled forward and set the phone on my desk. "What does that have to do with your pissed-off demeanor and the missed calls and texts?"

"She must have accidentally answered my FaceTime. She was on top of Antonio in a compromising position," I confessed, my voice barely above a whisper.

"Antonio would never do anything to betray you. There must be an explanation. Did you ask her or him?"

"No, I hung up and have avoided both of their calls," I admitted, the shame of my impulsive reaction weighing heavily on me.

He blew out a frustrated breath. "Massimo, this is me talking to you as your best friend, not your head enforcer—you're being stupid."

"Look," I said, pushing back from my desk. "I don't want to talk about it, okay? I need to find Juan Carlos and end this so I can go to Italy. If Madison has fallen for my brother, who is there for her when I can't be, I'll have no one to blame but myself. I made her go."

The room fell silent, the tension thick in the air. I could feel Donny's eyes on me, filled with a mixture of pity and concern. He knew as well as I did that the real battle wasn't just finding Juan Carlos; it was dealing with the mess I had created in my personal life.

"Well, I can help you with the Juan situation. Miguel has him —they are waiting in the basement."

"What? How?"

"It looks like Juan is not liked very much by his followers. It didn't take long for them to turn on him when they heard you were looking for him. Not to mention, Miguel offered the position of his second to the man who brought him in."

I snatched the phone from my desk and dialed my brother. "Vin…" I took a breath, trying to steady myself. "Our friend has arrived. Think you could come help me welcome him?"

"I'll be there in ten minutes." He disconnected the call abruptly, and I smiled. I knew he wouldn't just leave me to deal with him alone. Staring at my phone, I knew I needed to call Antonio back. It would be close to one in the morning in Italy, but he'd want to know the update.

"I thought you'd never call me." His voice was rough, telling me I'd woken him. "Look, Massimo, it's not what you—"

"I didn't call for that," I cut him off, my voice betraying a hint of desperation. "We finally have what we need, and I'll be able to take care of that issue that's been looming."

"What?" I heard his bed squeak, making me wonder if Madison was with him.

"Are you alone?" I bit out, jealousy clawing at my insides.

"What the fuck? Do you seriously think I'd do something like that to you? That woman loves you, brother. Get over yourself. If you think I'd be so low to fuck someone you love, you don't need my opinion on anything." The line went dead, leaving me stunned, a knot tightening in my chest.

He was right. Blood was always thicker than water. He'd never turn his back on me or betray me over a woman. Tossing my phone on my desk, I rested my elbows on the wood, burying my head in my hands. I stayed like that, the weight of my mistakes pressing down on me until Vincenzo found me.

"Fratello." He slammed the door, his gaze confused as he took in my less-than-stellar state. "I thought you'd be happier right now."

"I fucked up," I muttered, my voice barely audible.

"Fucked up? I thought you said you had Juan Carlos."

"I do... It's not that. I fucked up with Antonio...*and* Madison."

"What? I'm lost." He plopped down in the chair across from me, his brow furrowed in concern. "If this is about the alliance, we knew getting Juan would cost us."

"It's not the alliance—that matter is a done deal. You know the union with him opens pathways we normally wouldn't have."

"Then I am lost... what did you fuck up with Antonio?" He

studied me closely, his eyes narrowing. "Ah…I see. This is more about her and not him. Explain."

"I called him earlier, wanting to talk to Madison. The phone was answered by accident, and she was on top of him. I assumed the worst and hung up. When I just called him, he went off on me. He said if I thought that lowly of him, I didn't need to involve him in the family business."

"Massimo, you know he is more sensitive than you and me. I don't know why he has such low self-esteem, but whatever it is, it has him constantly battling to fit in. And you fucking know better." Vincenzo's voice rose an octave, his frustration palpable. "You need to go to Italy and fix this."

"First, we deal with Juan Carlos."

"No." Vincenzo stood up, his expression resolute. "I'll take care of him. You get the girl and fix this mess with our brother. His entire world is about to crash when Grandfather goes. He needs us, Massimo—both of us." I glanced at my watch. It would take me eleven hours if we didn't make any stops, putting me there at about two in the afternoon. The thought of seeing Madison, of fixing things with Antonio, filled me with a renewed sense of urgency.

"You sure?"

"Yes, go. You need her just as much as she needs you."

I patted his shoulder, appreciating his unwavering support, and pulled the door open. "Let's go tell our new partner it's time to end this."

Of course, as soon as I stepped into the hallway, I was bombarded by Investigator Holden from the D.A.'s office. He was pissed that he had yet to speak with Madison directly about the shooting at the college, but like the other three times, I told him she'd flown to Italy to be with my family. His sudden appearance was an interruption I didn't need when all I wanted was to get to Madison in Italy.

I felt torn between two worlds. My responsibility as the Don and the desire to see the woman I wanted.

As much as I'd been willing to leave Juan Carlos in the capable hands of my brother, it was my duty to see things through. Not to mention, I needed to see his eyes when he realized his people had turned on him. Before heading to my private plane, I'd stopped in and made sure Juan Carlos knew who he'd crossed. It had been bittersweet to hear him pleading for his life when I'd finally left him with my brother.

Vincenzo might have been known as a renowned chef, but he had a sick side to him, a past he'd fought to keep hidden. I knew letting his dark side out to play would make Juan's death painful.

The flight took longer than I wanted. We had to stop in Paris for fuel, making me antsy. By the time I got there, a full day had passed since my brother and I spoke on the phone— rather, he yelled at me before hanging up. Glancing at my screen, I worried my late arrival would be bothersome to everyone.

Speaking to my family's longtime driver in Italian, I leaned back in my seat and closed my eyes. I was exhausted from traveling. The time difference made me feel like I'd been beaten and dragged through town. It would be noon in Vegas, but it was nine in Italy, and I wondered if Madison was even awake. Knowing she wasn't speaking to me had me worried. I'd fucked up…bad.

When Aldo pulled into the driveway, my insides twisted with guilt. I opened the door before he stopped fully and hurried up the path to the front door. Gripping the knob, I took a deep breath and pushed inside.

Antonio stood at the bottom of the stairs with his arms folded over his chest, glaring at me. "Wow…a few minutes later, and you'd have caught me in bed with Madison."

"All right, I get it, brother." I held up my hands in defeat. "I fucked up."

"You think? How the hell could you think I would cross that line? I've come to love that girl like she's my sister, and you've hurt her in the worst possible way."

"I know. That's why I'm here."

He sighed, seeing my worried expression. "She hasn't come out of her room at all since your assumption was made, not to mention your avoidance of her calls."

"Antonio." I stepped close to him. "I'm sorry. I overreacted, and I regret what I've done. You were here for her when I couldn't be. It made me think she'd fallen for you instead."

"Are you serious?" He shook his head. "That girl is in love with you. Sure," he laughed, and the sound was music to my ears, "she needed time to come to terms with loving an asshole, but she did. Now…" He stepped closer. "Are you going to fix it or what? I want her in this family, and so do the others."

"Me, too." I tugged him against me. "I love you, fratello."

Antonio hugged me back. "Go see her."

"Thank you for taking care of her."

Smiling, I took the stairs two at a time. When I stopped outside her room, her door was closed. Pressing my hand on the wood, I leaned my head against the cool surface and listened. Even through the barrier, I could hear her whimpers, and the sound nearly crushed my soul.

Easing the door open, I stepped into the darkness. Even in the blackened room, I could make out her form on the bed. The soft moonlight bathed her shape beneath the covers in a soft glow. As my eyes adjusted, I could see the soft shaking of her sobs.

"'Leave me alone, Antonio," she whispered into the darkness.

Kicking my shoes off, I undressed and crept to her bedside. Easing the covers back, I slipped in beside her and wrapped my body around hers. She tensed as I pressed a kiss to her neck. "I'm so sorry, baby. The way I acted by not answering your calls was wrong. I jumped to the wrong conclusion because I thought you'd fallen for Antonio."

She rolled over to look at me. Her face was red and swollen. Pressing my thumb to her cheek, I wiped the tears dripping down her skin as she spoke. "I haven't fallen for your brother. He's important to me. We've shared things that haunt us, bringing us close. But Massimo…" She sucked in a breath. "I love you. I thought…" She hiccupped a sob. "I thought you changed your mind about us."

"Changing my mind was never an option once I found you, bella." I leaned forward and kissed away her tears. "I thought it was you who'd changed your mind. Can you forgive me?" I brushed the hair away from her face and cupped her cheek.

"You need to make it right with Antonio. He has so much that he's dealing with, Massimo. Losing your grandfather is going to shatter him. He needs you."

"I know. He's part of the reason I came. What do you mean, he has so much he's dealing with?"

"It's not my story to tell." Madison pressed her hand against my chest. "Just know when the time comes, and he's ready to share. Show him unconditional love."

I didn't know what that meant, but it made my heart swell with even more love for her. "He's my brother. Whatever burden he is carrying, I'll lift it for him, no matter what. You didn't answer me, though." I pulled her tighter against my body." Can you forgive me, bella?"

"Of course, I forgive you. You came here." She smiled. "Wait…if you're here, does that mean you've taken care of the issue?"

"Vincenzo has most likely disposed of the matter by now. I left him to take care of the final problem."

She tilted her head and held my gaze. "You didn't stay to—I dunno oversee that?"

""Madison…" I threaded my fingers into her hair. "I know it's been a short amount of time, but I would've moved heaven and earth to get to you. You own me."

I captured her lips, giving her proof of that ownership. Her body relaxed against me as we melted into one.

twenty-three

MADISON

HE WAS HERE.

Massimo had come for me.

"You're wearing my shirt." He tugged at the dress shirt I had on.

A blush crept up my skin as I hid my face against his chest and spoke. "It made me feel close to you."

"As sexy as it looks on you, it needs to be off." Massimo tugged it over my head and tossed it behind him to the floor. My breasts bounced free, and I attempted to cover them, but he grabbed my hands and pulled them free. His head descended on them, sucking my nipple into his mouth while his free hand palmed the other. I moaned, grinding my hips into his rock-hard penis.

"Fuck, bella." he licked across my flesh, nipping the other nipple as I writhed beneath his muscular body.

"These need to go, too." He snagged the tiny lace panties covering my center and ripped them off. I pawed at Massimo's boxers, pushing them down his hips, causing his very nice dick to spring free. Tentatively, I reached between our bodies and wrapped my hand around him.

"Please, Massimo," she begged. "I need you inside me."

Fisting his cock, I jerked my palm up and down the steel-hard shaft. Massimo grunted as his eyes closed in pleasure. I wasn't sure if I was doing it right, but when he rolled on top of me, fitting his body between my thighs, I knew he wanted me.

Wrapping my legs around his back, I silently begged him to consume me. I couldn't hold back my scream of pleasure as he drove himself inside me. He filled me to the brim, touching parts of me I never knew existed. Even though he was well endowed, it was like he was made for me. He froze once he was seated fully, his ass clenching beneath my heels.

"Fuck, bella. Your pussy feels so good."

My body was on fire from his touch. Massimo pumped his cock in and out of my channel, his rhythm absolute perfection. He adjusted his angle, placing his hand beneath my ass and lifting me. Bracing himself on the bed, he pumped harder and faster as if he were a possessed man or perhaps a man trying to possess me.

The sensation built, starting in my toes. I couldn't have stopped the moan of pleasure bursting from my lips if I tried. Clawing at his back, I eagerly pulled him closer as he pounded into me. His head dipped, and he caught my nipple between his teeth. The feeling of his lips against my flesh drew another orgasm from my body. Arching against him, I pushed my hips up, begging him to send me over the edge one more time.

"I'm close, baby. Can you give me one more?" he murmured against my flesh.

I nodded, unable to form words. Slipping his hand from beneath me, he eased it between our bodies. His finger swirled around my clit before he pinched the swollen nub in his fingers. Lights danced across my eyes as the most powerful release flooded my senses. I could feel my juices coating his dick as my pussy clamped down on his rigid member. His body tensed as his movements became jerky. My center filled with warmth as his cock exploded inside me, coating my walls with his seed.

"Goddamn." Massimo rested his forehead against mine as his body stilled above me. His warm breath brushed against my face as I pressed my lips to his, my tongue plundering his mouth in ecstasy.

"I love you, Massimo."

"Good." He kissed a trail down my face and nibbled my neck beneath my ear. "Because I don't think I could let you go."

He rolled off me, his semi-hard cock slipping from between my folds, and tucked me against his body. "I am sorry for hurting you, bella. My jealousy got the better of me."

"Honestly, I would've felt the same if I'd seen something like that. You and Antonio, okay?"

"I think so. You and he have become close. I see that now.."

I glanced over my shoulder at him. "You don't have to be jealous, though. Like I told you, he and I connected in a way that differs from you and me. Antonio is trying to figure out where he belongs, and I understand what that's like."

"Belongs?" Massimo pressed his lips to my neck. "He's an Anastasi—"

"You should have this conversation with him, not me."

"Okay. Maybe you'll be good for the whole family. You balance me and have helped Antonio in a way I obviously can't. What do you think of the rest of my family?"

"Your parents are the sweetest people I've ever met. It's hard to believe your dad is the head of a crime family. Your sisters are hysterical, and I can't wait for them to move to Vegas."

"Does it bother you what I do for the family in Vegas?"

"At first, it did, but after talking with Antonio, I realize you'll protect me and your family at all costs. That's not something I've not had in a long time."

"I would never let anything happen to you. I'd give my own life to spare yours."

Rolling to face him, I cupped his cheek. "How about you just live for me and love me?"

"I'll love you until the end of time, Madison. You have my heart in your hands. It is you that has the power to destroy me. Never forget that."

"Me?" I ran my fingers through his hair. "I'm only a girl. You're a man with so much at his disposal. How could I destroy you?"

"If you ever left me, you'd take my beating heart. The air that I breathe exists because you're near me. Without you, I've realized I'm an incomplete man. Take you away, and I have nothing…not even myself."

"How did I get so lucky to find you?" A tear slipped down my cheek.

"It's me who's lucky."

Melding our lips together, I felt the familiar desire pooling in my belly. This man thought I had power over him, but he brought me to my knees with a simple look or touch.

"You make me wanton with need, bella." His erection dug into my belly as we kissed and touched. Being apart made me realize how much I needed him in my world.

"Take me to the shower." I pressed a kiss to his jaw, sucking the tender flesh.

Massimo moved quickly, pulling me into his arms as he carried us both to the bathroom. He deposited me on the counter and turned on the showerheads. Watching Massimo's nude body move around the massive enclosure made my insides ache with need all over again. Although he had been my first, I couldn't imagine anyone ever comparing to him. The way my body responded to him made me believe he was made for me.

After scooping me off the vanity, he carried me into the stall. The mist warmed my skin as he held me beneath the spray.

My legs wrapped securely around his waist as he held me close to his chest. Our lips melted together, the passion lighting the flame of need inside us.

Massimo sat down on the bench, my legs resting on either side of him. My core was poised over the head of his cock, making it easy to slip him inside me. My vagina wrapped around his shaft as he burrowed deep inside my womb. When he flexed his hips, my walls spasmed around his dick, drawing a guttural moan from his throat.

We were lost in the rhythm of our love as the water surrounded us with a mist of lust. Every fiber was firing on heat and desire, causing my whole body to quake with an explosive orgasm. I screamed out, leaning my head back into the water. Massimo sucked my nipple into his mouth, licking and biting the pink flesh.

"I can't hold on, baby. Come with me one more time."

Bouncing, I flexed my legs and rubbed my clit against his pubic bone. My nub was swollen and needy, begging for release. He thrust up into me, ramming himself against my cervix. His eyes squeezed shut as his breathing became erratic. He was just as close as I was. Like a flash of light, our bodies exploded in a feverish climax. My center clamped down on his shaft, forcing every ounce of his seed from him. Collapsing against him, I rested my head in the crook of his neck. He eased me off him, sitting me on the bench beside him.

"Wait here, bella. I'm going to clean you up and get us back to bed."

My eyes fluttered closed as he wiped the evidence of our coupling from my legs. I vaguely remember him wrapping a towel around me and carrying me to the bed. His body eased in behind me, the covers draped over our bodies as he held me against him.

In his arms, I felt as if I could conquer anything.

twenty-four

MASSIMO

I LEFT Madison asleep in bed as I crept down the hallway. She needed to rest, and I still had to resolve some things between Antonio and me. Rounding the corner, I was surprised to find my grandmother sitting at the table.

"Nonna… What are you doing here?" I smiled as I spoke in Italian. I quickly realized her expression did not reciprocate my happiness. "Is it Grandfather?"

"Yes," she sighed, her eyes shining with unshed tears. Her accent was thick with remorse and sadness. "Giuseppe has gone to the angels, Massimo. Your father is at the hospital making the arrangements."

"Where is Antonio?" I looked around, noticing how quiet the house was.

"He ran out of the house when I told him. He is somewhere on the grounds. I knew this would be hard on him. Your grandfather understood him in a way your father does not. It will take time for him to open up to you. Although," she forced a small grin, "your bride-to-be seems to have bonded to him."

"Bride-to-be?" I scratched my head. "Madison? I have not asked her yet, Nonna. I take it you met her?"

"Yes. She sat at the hospital with Giuseppe and me. She is a lovely woman and will be a great addition to the Anastasi name. You are asking her to marry you?"

"Of course."

"Maybe a funeral first." She wiped a lone tear from her face. "Then a wedding will bring us out of despair."

"I don't know if she will say yes."

"Yes, you do." Madison's voice filled the room. She walked up behind me and wrapped her arms around my middle. "I love you, Massimo, plus no one tells you no."

"I don't doubt your love." Pulling her around to my front, I held her in my arms and rested my head on top of hers. "I just wanted to ask you the right way."

"Vittoria." She tilted her head at my grandmother. "I am sorry about Giuseppe. I wish I could have met him before this happened. He sounds like a wonderful man who loved his family."

"He was. He would have approved of you." Her English was broken but filled with such kindness.

"What can I do for you?" Madison reached out and took her hand in hers.

"Nothing, sweet girl. Look after Massimo and my other grandsons."

"Oh, God! Antonio?" She turned toward me with wide eyes. "Where is he?"

She sighed. "The gardens. He has not come in since I told him."

"Can I?" She paused, looking at me for permission. "Massimo, would you mind if I went to check on him?"

"Actually, we can go together. You were right last night. I need to be there for him now. Nonna." I leaned down and pressed a kiss to her head. "Will you be all right for a moment?"

"Yes. I said my goodbyes some time ago. I think Giuseppe was waiting for her." She pointed to Madison.

She jerked back, confused. "Me?"

"Yes. He knew Massimo would need a strong woman to balance him now that he is to lead the family in the United States. I believe he could hear you talking and knew his time had come. You set them both free, Madison. Now, find Antonio. He will be lost for some time, but I think you will help him."

Madison embraced my grandmother, her tears staining the silken shirt she wore. "I will take care of them all. You have my word."

"Come." I tugged her hand and led her to the gardens in the back. "Let's find Antonio. I need him to know I am here for him, and there's nothing he could say or do that would change that."

"I hope you're serious. When he finds the strength to tell you his burdens, he will need your support. Don't forget he is still your brother when that time comes."

I mulled over her words, wondering what secret he held that made him feel so terrible. There was nothing that would change the fact he was an Anastasi. The same blood that ran through his veins ran through mine.

I halted our steps, pulling Madison to a stop.

"Thank you, Madison."

"For what?"

"Being there for him when I couldn't. I'm glad you and Antonio are so close. If he won't talk to me, it comforts me to know that he has you."

"Well, that's a good thing because this whole dang family has burrowed its way into my heart. Even Vincenzo, as scary as he is."

"We won't be leaving Italy for a while. Are you okay with that?"

"Yes. We need to be here for the family."

I pressed her knuckles to my lips and kissed the delicate flesh. Her beauty wasn't just external but deep within her soul. "How did I get so lucky to find you, bella?"

"You took a gamble on me—and won your bet."

She leaned into my side as we went in search of my brother. I didn't know what secrets he was harboring but knowing that Madison was there for him was good enough for me.

twenty-five
MADISON

SURREAL.

That's the only way to describe the number of people who turned out for Giuseppe's funeral. He was a man many people respected. Massimo had warned me the service would be large, but nothing could have prepared me for the actual day. Antonio had insisted on helping me dress, ensuring I was decked out in only the best fashion. I thought it was silly, but letting him have his fun seemed to help him bury the grief I knew he was consumed with.

No matter what I said to him, he was not ready to discuss what made him feel so lonely. I insisted he was wrong about how the others would react, but he didn't want to hear it. In the end, I dropped the conversation, telling him I would be there when he was ready to tell everyone. I loved him like a brother and would do anything to prevent his hurt.

Vincenzo was different from what I initially thought. Sure, he was definitely scary, but since arriving, he'd done nothing but treat me like his sister and vowed to protect me forever. Plus, he promised me all the free food I wanted.

I learned a lot by just listening to conversations between the family and all the visitors. Several men refer to Vincenzo as The Lama, which I knew was Italian for the blade. I suspected it had nothing to do with being a cook, but I didn't ask.

Catarina, the oldest of the girls, arrived with Vincenzo in Italy when their grandfather passed. She had confided in me that she had wanted something different from the typical family business, but being a nurse meant she had to deal with the medical issues they encountered. She laughed and said she'd been more involved as a nurse than she intended. She joked that stitching up the guys was a regular thing, and I better get used to it.

Massimo was standing with several men who made the godfather from the movies look like Barney. He patted one of them on the back, then pulled him into a hug. I couldn't hear him, but he said something, causing all of them to look my way. Blushing, I waved, unsure of how to respond. My gut churned with unease as they drew closer.

"Madison." Massimo held out his hand, urging me to join them. "I'd like you to meet Filippo Bianchi. His family are longtime friends—and an ally to our family." Massimo smiled at the man.

"Hello, Mr. Bianchi." I held out my hand, allowing him to press a gentle kiss against my knuckles.

"No, no. Call me Filippo. You are a beautiful lady. What is someone as gorgeous as you doing with this oaf?"

I stiffened at his laughter, cutting my eyes toward Massimo, who simply winked. "It took some convincing, but I think I've persuaded her to give me a chance."

"Well," Filippo grinned, "if you ever tire of him, call me. I'd make you my queen."

"There will be no need." Massimo stepped behind me and pulled me flush to his front. "Madison is already a queen."

"Thank you, Filippo, but Massimo is being dramatic. I am no queen. I am, however, his."

We exchanged a few more words before Massimo ushered me off to look for his grandmother, who'd disappeared into a private room. She was sitting alone at the window, staring at the landscape beyond the glass, lost in a world of her own.

"Nonna?" Massimo tilted his head, concern marring his face. "Are you all right?"

She turned slowly, her eyes filled with a sadness that seemed to have deepened over the years. "Massimo, my dear. I'm just… reminiscing."

"Why don't you go get us some drinks?" I patted his cheek and leaned in to press a kiss to his tender skin. "I'll go talk to Vittoria."

Massimo nodded reluctantly and left the room, his shoulders tense with worry. I moved slowly toward Vittoria, my heart aching for the sadness etched into her features. I pressed my hand to her shoulder, and she glanced back, finally realizing someone was in the room with her.

"Madison." Her accent was thick with sorrow. "Why are you not with Massimo?"

"We came to check on you. He has gone to fetch some drinks," I explained softly, taking a seat beside her.

"Pfft. I'm fine. You two should be out there celebrating Giuseppe's life, not in here with a sad, old woman."

"I'd rather be in here with you than out there pretending to smile at all those strangers," I said earnestly. "Besides, you knew Giuseppe better than anyone. I want to hear about him from you."

A faint smile touched her lips. "You are a good woman." She patted my leg as I sat across from her. "When will you marry my grandson?"

I coughed, caught off guard by her directness. "We've only known each other a short time, Vittoria."

"Giuseppe and I met when I was eighteen. I knew immediately he was the man I would spend forever with. Three days later, I was his wife. We had sixty-eight wonderful years together, and I will treasure every memory made."

"Three days?" I echoed, astonished. "That's incredible. How did you know?"

"Yes. Madison, the heart knows when it finds who it is meant for. Can you imagine a life without Massimo?"

I looked toward the closed door, wishing he'd come back. "No... I can't, but I'm scared. Everything is happening so fast."

"Fear is a silly emotion. We cannot stop fate, sweet girl. Letting uncertainty rule you will only lead to heartache in the end," she said, her eyes searching mine with a knowing look.

"Well… it doesn't matter until he asks me," I murmured, feeling the weight of her words.

"Asks you what?" Massimo's voice filled the room, causing me to startle. He had returned quietly, carrying two glasses of wine.

"Nothing." I smiled, embarrassed that he had probably heard us talking.

"We were talking about when you two will marry. I want to fill this house with happiness… Giuseppe would want that." She pulled at her fingers and reached out to Massimo, handing him something. "Here, I want you to have this."

Massimo set down the drink he was holding and opened his hand. She placed it in his palm, causing him to look up at her with wide eyes. Vittoria had removed the glittering diamond from her left hand and given it to him.

"Nonna, I can't take this."

"You can and you will. Now, give it to this girl. I want a wedding soon." She pushed up from the bench and gave a half-hearted smile. "I'll leave you two to chat."

Massimo hugged her tightly. "Nonna, I love you."

"I know, boy. Make her yours." She winked at me as she slowly made her way out of the room.

I watched as the door closed behind her, my heart pounding. "What just happened?"

"I think my Nonna has just given me an order." Massimo chuckled, setting down the glass he held in his other hand. He moved to stand in front of me and squatted.

"Massimo?" I asked, confused and overwhelmed by what he was doing.

"Madison, this is not the way I planned on doing this, but Nonna is right. When you know, you know…" He dropped to one knee, causing me to cover my mouth with my hands and gasp.

"You walked into my casino like a thunderous freight train. I knew in that instant I would make you mine. You ground me in ways I never thought possible. It's like you are the lighthouse high on the rocks in the middle of a storm, and I'm the lowly ship being guided to you. Wherever you are, I want to be. After three days, Nonna knew Giuseppe was her soul mate. Until you, I never thought they existed. I know you're scared of how you feel. Hell, I am, too, but I cannot imagine being without you in this life or the next. Will you take a chance on me and do me the honor of becoming my goddess?"

"Massimo…" I ran my hand down his face, cupping his cheek in my hand. Tears welled in my eyes as I nodded. "Yes. I will marry you."

Standing, he captured my lips in a passionate kiss, his fingers lacing into my hair. I tugged his shoulders, drawing our bodies closer, feeling his heartbeat echoing my own. Breaking the kiss, he held out the engagement ring that had been on his grandmother's finger moments before. Carefully easing it onto my ring finger, he smiled once it was seated.

"It fits." He grinned even wider, his eyes sparkling with joy. "This is proof we're meant to be. I love you, Madison. You own my soul."

"I love you too, Massimo," I whispered, still marveling at the ring on my finger. "I can't believe this is happening."

"It's real, bella. And it's just the beginning."

MASSIMO

THIS WAS SUPPOSED to be our moment—she'd agreed to be my wife. The moment Vincenzo burst through the door, I knew something was wrong.

"Vincenzo." I turned to face him. "What is it?" Madison tucked herself under my arm, pressing into my side.

"We have a problem, fratello."

I stiffened at his words. "What do you mean, a problem?"

He glanced toward Madison. "One of the women I *see* was found dead on my doorstep by one of the guards."

"I don't understand." I held Madison against me, my fingers absently brushing against her arm. "Have the men clean it up, and we will deal with it when we get home."

He covered his face with his palm and blew out a breath. "We can't. The police are at my house now, and based on who it was, they are going to be gunning for my head."

I tensed. "Why is that, fratello?"

"Because the dead girl is the police chief's daughter."

"Fuck." I closed my eyes and took a deep breath. I turned to Madison. "I'm sorry. I wanted to spend time here, with you, but…"

She pressed her hand to my cheek. "I understand. We need to go home. When I said yes to you, I knew this was part of the deal."

"Wait…" Vincenzo grabbed her hand. "You asked her?"

"Yes." I ran my hand through my hair. "Right before you walked in."

"Oh my God." He tugged her from my hold and embraced her. "Welcome to the family."

"You can let go now." I yanked him back. "Go get Antonio. We need to tell father what's going on and get back to Vegas ASAP."

"I'll take care of that. You," Vincenzo pointed to me, "need to go tell Nonna the good news. Mom and Dad as well."

"You're right. Take care of the arrangements. Madison and I will tell everyone our surprise." I laced my fingers in hers. "Vincenzo?" I cocked a brow at him as we walked toward the door. "Why would they think you did this?"

"She was, uh…" He paused at the door. "Found bound, gagged, and had marks that indicated she'd been whipped." Vincenzo glanced toward Madison. His eyes held embarrassment.

"What the fuck? Are you saying it was staged to look like you were role-playing?"

"Yes, but I swear to you, I've never seen this girl before. Hell," he walked into the hallway, "I was here when her death happened. The chief won't listen to reason. He is blinded by rage and wants my head."

"We'll fix this. Surely, he will see the stupidity of blaming you. The question is…" I paused. "Who would want to set us up like this?"

"That's the million-dollar question."

"Don't worry." I patted him on the back. "We'll get this sorted out."

Vincenzo nodded and walked away, leaving Madison and me alone. "Are you sure you still want to marry me? This is what life will be like."

"Stop doubting how I feel about you. Am I scared…yes. But I know you'll protect me above all else. Let's go." She grabbed my hand. "The sooner we tell everyone, the sooner we can return to Vegas and get this sorted out. I don't enjoy seeing Vincenzo so…" She paused. "Worried."

Her words resonated with me. She was right. Vincenzo seemed scared, something he rarely was. He was skilled with a blade, earning him the nickname La Lama. A skill that had nothing to do with being a chef. "You're right. He was worried."

"Vincenzo has a side few know about." Madison looked into my eyes, and a realization dawned. "A side he'd rather not have advertised. So whoever did this knows about his tastes.

Antonio is not the only one with demons. The club allows Vincenzo a way to expel his."

"Demons?"

"Just like you once said to me, it is his story to tell. Maybe one day he'll open up to you, as Antonio did. Know this, though—Vincenzo is a good man."

"Of course he is. This doesn't change my opinion of him."

We made our way out to the others and explained why we were leaving. My father offered to call the chief himself, knowing that his son's freedom was at stake. It was surreal piling into the plane with my siblings and soon-to-be wife. The strangest thing was seeing my tough brother so beaten down.

"Has Donny found anything?" Vincenzo rested his hands on his knees, his head bowed in defeat.

"No. The cameras were disabled…cut, actually. So, there's no footage of anyone entering the property. What I do know is she was not killed there—her body had been staged."

"Fuck," he murmured.

The plane touched down after fourteen hours, and I ushered us all off to the awaiting cars. Donny was standing by one of the SUVs, waiting for us. Freddy stood by the second one, smiling as we approached.

"Maddie." He pulled her into a hug, then turned to me. "I'm glad to see you back. Mr. Anastasi."

"Freddy, you'll be driving my brothers. Madison and I will ride with Donny."

"Yes, sir." He turned toward me. "I'll be seeing you, Maddie."

"It's Madison," Massimo barked.

"Oh…yes, Sir, my apologies."

"It's fine, Freddy. You can call me Maddie. Massimo is just being…" She raised a brow. "A jerk." She brushed past me, bumping into my shoulder as she climbed into the backseat.

"Oh, she's going to keep you on your toes." Donny snickered as he climbed into the driver's seat.

"You're probably right." I slid into the seat beside Madison and tugged the door closed. Unable to resist touching her, I laced my fingers with hers. She cocked an eyebrow as I tugged her hand to my lips and placed a gentle kiss on her knuckles. We pulled down the alley behind the club, the interior silent as Donny cut off the engine.

"Madison." I turned toward Madison, but she put my finger to my lips.

"Shhh, I know. I'll go to the apartment and wait. If something happens, have Carlisle come and get me."

"Thank you. I wouldn't be able to focus if you were there."

"It's okay. I know there will be times when I cannot be a part of your life. Just come back to me." She leaned in and kissed me. "I'll be upstairs taking a bath."

I groaned, adjusting myself as I slid out behind her. "Now I'm going to have that image in my brain. Maybe you should come with me."

"Boss." Donny held the door open. "The chief is waiting for you in the office. Antonio and Vincenzo are already with him." Looked like my father's influence still mattered. Even from Sicily, he was able to call in some favors. "I also asked Miguel to be here—he might have some insight we don't."

"Bella." Madison turned to my voice. "I'll be up soon." I pulled her against me, my mouth finding hers.

"Be safe." She turned, giving me a flirtatious grin as she stepped through the door. "I'll be waiting…"

I turned toward the front of the club as Madison called out over her shoulder, "Naked."

I forced myself to my office despite the raging desire to chase after Madison. As soon as I stepped in, Harold Larson, the chief of police, spoke.

"We have a problem."

Vincenzo was seated in a chair, and Antonio stood with arms folded behind him against the wall.

"We do, but I can assure you that it wasn't us."

"I've come to realize that in talking with Vincenzo. Besides, he was in Italy with your family. My condolences for your loss."

"Thank you, but this means we have a problem that affects us both."

"Yes, my daughter…" His voice faltered. "My daughter was a beautiful creature; sure, she was a bit wild, but she did not deserve the death she was given."

"Are you sure it wasn't someone inside the Sureños?" I turned my gaze to Miguel, who was standing and listening.

"No, I've taken care of any uncertain loyalties. The only ones who remain are loyal to me and support our alliance."

"Why me? I don't understand." Vincenzo's tone was bitter with hate.

"I think someone is trying to flush you out of hiding, my friend." Miguel sneered. "You are The Lama, are you not?"

Antonio hissed behind Vincenzo before uttering what we were all thinking. It had been a few years since anyone outside the family had spoken that name. Vincenzo worked hard to bury that part of himself and hearing it from Miguel's lips made me cringe.

Vincenzo growled, his eyes narrowing on Miguel, who simply shrugged. "It is you," Miguel inched closer, his eyes burrowing into Vincenzo's soul, "is it not?"

"What am I missing?" the chief asked, and his confused eyes scanned the room. "I thought the La Lama was just folklore—a made-up monster that doesn't exist."

"He doesn't exist. Not anymore." Vincenzo's teeth clenched together. "It's best if we forget about him."

"It seems someone wants you to remember." Miguel clicked his tongue against his teeth. "We must figure out who would want to bring the dead back to life.'"

"Vincenzo." I pressed my hand against his shoulder. "We're going to need the names of every job you worked."

"Massimo…" His voice cracked as he spoke. "Please, I've worked hard to leave that part of me in the dark. If you make me do this, you'll be opening Pandora's Box."

"My daughter deserves the truth. And if you don't help me, I'll expose your entire family—I don't care what kind of agreement we have."

"Look." Vin cleared his throat. "If I go back to that place, and it turns out it has nothing to do with me, then what? I would open myself up to speculation. We don't need the feds getting wind that The Lama has returned. It's dangerous for both organizations." He pinned the chief of police with a glare that made him visibly shiver.

"He's right," Antonio said, pushing off the wall. "What happens when the people above your paygrade get wind that someone is poking around and asking questions about The Lama? They'll start sniffing around again, tying him to old crimes we've buried. Crimes you helped cover up, chief."

He stood. "My life means nothing if I can't avenge my flesh and blood. Burning your family to the ground might not bring her back, but you'd no longer have someone in your pocket because I'd be in prison. I imagine you have more to lose than me."

"It is a necessary risk. Whoever did this is threatening all of us," Miguel growled. "We have too much at stake to just ignore it."

"Vincenzo." I rubbed my forehead. "We need to do this. It's a risk we need to take." I could see the strain on his face as he mulled over my words.

"Fine."

"Great." Miguel moved toward the door. "I'll send only my trusted men. They will help you with this search. Your daughter did not deserve to be humiliated like that. Seems someone has it out for Vincenzo and is doing their best to expose the family, using him."

"Are you sure it wasn't a jilted lover?" Vincenzo asked. "What if this was someone trying to start a war between us and your department?"

"It was no lover. My daughter was not into things…like that.." He stood and headed toward the door. "Find who did this, Anastasi. Because my freedom means nothing compared to yours."

twenty-seven

MASSIMO

ONE MONTH HAD PASSED since the chief's daughter was found murdered outside Vincenzo's house, and we still had no leads. The image of her lifeless body haunted me, a constant reminder of our failure. Most of the kill contracts Vincenzo had fulfilled for my father as La Lama, were on the up and up. No one seemed to hold a grudge or wanted vengeance. Yet, the uncertainty gnawed at me. Vincenzo was spending more and more time at the club, neglecting his business. He'd agreed to hire someone to manage it, but it was turning out to add more stress than relief. He'd refused every candidate he'd interviewed so far, leaving him more agitated than before.

Antonio was taking on the burden of handling Miguel and his men, easing some of the pressure of our alliance with the Mexican mafia. Meanwhile, Madison had stepped up as the assistant manager of the club. Since she'd earned her degree early—from the hefty donation and strongly worded suggestion I'd made to the dean of her college, I decided she was better suited for the role, and frankly, I didn't want other men ogling what was mine.

I was lost in these thoughts when Madison's voice pierced through my reverie.

"You look deep in thought," she said, her tone soft yet curious.

I snapped back to the present, meeting her eyes. "Thinking about my beautiful fiancée."

"Really?" She arched an eyebrow, a playful smirk on her lips as she stepped into my office. "Is she hot?"

I stood, closing the distance between us. Her presence was magnetic, drawing me in. I kicked the door closed behind her and traced a finger down her neck, savoring the warmth of her skin.

"So. Fucking. Hot," I whispered, my voice thick with desire.

Our lips met in a fierce kiss, a clash of passion and possession. Madison's arms wrapped around my neck, pulling me closer as I deepened the kiss, my need for her consuming every thought. I walked us backward, pressing her against the office door. Her tiny dress rode up her thighs, exposing her to me. The thin lace of her panties was the only barrier between us, and in one swift jerk, I tore the fabric away, letting it fall to the ground.

"It's going to get expensive if you keep ripping my panties off."

"Maybe you should just go commando." As I lifted her further up the wall, her legs locked around my waist, her hips grinding into me and begging me to take her. "What do you want, bella?"

"Massimo," she whispered, her voice trembling with anticipation.

I popped the button on my pants, freeing myself from the confines of my boxers, and eased myself inside her. The warmth of her center wrapped around my erection, causing me to groan in pleasure.

"Fuck." My hips pushed forward on their own free will. I leaned over her, my lips brushing against her ear. "I'm going to make you forget everything else," I promised, my hands already exploring her body.

Madison moaned, the sound making me mad with lust. My cock took over. It pulsed inside of her, demanding for me to move. I ground into her, rubbing my pelvis against her swollen clit. Anyone walking by the office would know what was happening inside as her cries filled the space. It didn't matter. I wanted to own her pussy—show her I was in control. The door rattled with each flex of my body.

Her back was pressed firmly against it as I drove my cock in and out of her pussy. She fisted my hair, holding on as I ravished her, making us one at that moment. Our bodies tensed, our releases bursting from our souls at the exact moment. Her head fell against my shoulder, her breath coming out in pants.

"Jeepers." She giggled breathlessly, and I couldn't help but smile. Madison hardly ever swore, making her the ying to my yang. Her silly words were refreshing among the darkness that seemed to swirl around my life constantly. "I don't remember the real reason I came in here now."

"This was a good enough one for me." I pressed a kiss to her forehead as I helped her to her feet.

A knock sounded on the door behind her, causing her to jump. "Oh, shoot," Her face reddened in embarrassment. "I bet everyone knows what just happened in here."

"Relax." I pulled her against me. "No one is brave enough to say anything. If they do, I'll kill them."

Madison hurried to right herself before sitting down in a chair. I tucked myself back into my pants and smoothed out my shirt. Shaking off the lust haze, I opened the door.

"This better be fucking important."

"Sorry, boss." Donny stood in the hallway. "There's been another incident."

"Where?" I opened the door wider and ushered him inside.

Donny glanced at Madison, his face blushing with a knowing grin. "Maddie, how are you?"

"Piss off, Donny. Don't pretend you weren't standing outside the door when Massimo had his dick buried inside of me."

Donny glanced back at me. "She's getting feisty."

"She is." I walked around him to take my seat behind the desk. "Now, tell me what happened."

"There has been another attempt made."

"Attempt?" I rested my elbows on the surface of my desk and leaned forward. I couldn't help but notice Madison tensing beside him.

"Yes. It appears someone tried to grab your sister in the ER parking lot."

"Oh my God. Catarina!" Madison gasped as she pushed to her feet. "Is she hurt?"

"A few scratches. Vincenzo is with her. I came to tell you in person. He didn't feel a phone call would suffice."

"Motherfucker. Do we know who?"

"No. He was wearing a mask, and Catarina didn't get a good look. He tried to shove her into her car, but she fought him off. Someone passing by overheard the commotion and called security."

"The police are involved." It was a statement. Involving the cops brought more suspicion to our family, but sometimes it was unavoidable.

"Yes. They are at the restaurant right now. Catarina asked Vincenzo to take her there. Antonio stayed on the scene to speak with the officer. He's going to get what he can from their investigation. The paramedics cleared Catarina to leave, so she's fine, Massimo. Just a little shook up."

"Take me to her." I pushed back from my desk and stood.

"I want to go, too," Madison said, standing on her perch.

"Baby, I need you safe. Please stay here with Carlisle."

"No. Catarina is going to be my family soon. I want to go. Either I go with you, or I'll call Freddy to take me. If you stop him, I can always call an Uber."

"Fine. Donny, let's go." I motioned toward the door.

We hurried to the alley where the SUV was waiting. Piling into the backseat, I tugged Madison's hand into mine. I needed her touch to calm the rage boiling beneath the surface.

"Have you called Miguel? I want him to be aware of the incident. We need to put heat on some people and figure out who's out to get the family. I'm realizing this isn't just about digging up Vincenzo's ghosts." I took a deep breath. "This is about the whole organization."

"I'll call him when we get there."

"It'll be okay." Madison rubbed her thumb across the top of my hand. "You'll figure this out."

Remembering she had come into the office to tell me something, but my lust for her took over, I grinned at her. "What did you want earlier?"

"You mean before we gave Donny a show?"

Donny coughed. "I swear I wasn't out in the hall the whole time, Madison."

"I know. I just like making you squirm." She tugged my hand.

"Yes, bella. Before I marked you as mine again."

"It's not important right now. Your sister is all that matters at this moment. What I wanted to tell you can wait."

"No, tell me. You are just as important as any member of my family."

"'Just focus on Catarina." She leaned in and pressed a kiss to my lips as the SUV came to a stop. Pushing her door open, she climbed out, leaving me to stare at her behind. "My stuff can wait."

"You won the lottery with that one, Massimo. She's a real treasure, and I'm glad she's going to be part of the family."

"Me, too." We climbed from the SUV, and the three of us headed inside to find Vincenzo interrogating Catarina.

"Can you tell us anything else about him? Height, accent, anything?" Vincenzo spat. His temper was palpitating throughout the room when we stepped inside.

"No, Vincenzo. I told you. The man, and yes, I am certain it was a man, grabbed me from behind. He tried to force me into the passenger seat of my car, but I kicked him in the dick. He grabbed my shirt, ripping it." She waved at the material, which hung loosely, exposing her tattoos beneath. She was covered in beautiful artwork, spanning her entire chest and arms. Catarina usually kept them covered for work, but now, she was exposed for all to see.

Donny growled as he moved to stand beside her. "Here." He slipped off his jacket and handed it to her. "Put this on."

"Thanks," she whispered, her eyes looking at the floor in embarrassment.

"Don't." Donny grabbed her chin. "Never be ashamed, Cat. These people will be found, and this man will pay for what he did to you. Do you understand?"

She held his gaze. "Yes."

I glanced at the way my best friend was holding my sister. "Donny," I barked, making him step back and let go of her face. I want you to stay with Catarina and personally guard her."

"Me?" Donny looked shocked. "Shouldn't we put someone else on this detail? You need me to flush out information."

"I need her protection more. I trust you like one of my brothers. Knowing she is with you will give me some peace right now."

Catarina glanced between the two of them.

"I don't need a babysitter, Massimo. I've worked my whole life to put some distance between our family and my career. Having him around will undo all of it."

"I don't care. Someone tried to kidnap you, Cat. Do you understand that?" I was doing my best to reign in my anger, but the thought of having to bury a sibling had me near the point of letting out the full weight of being the Don. "If you hadn't gotten away, I'd be calling Mom and Dad to tell them you were gone. *Please*. Do this for me."

"Fine." She sighed. "Whatever. But this isn't going to be forever. And we," she turned to Donny, "will have to set some rules."

"I like rules." His eyes glinted with mischief as he chuckled. "I will be wherever you are. In fact, we should go now. I need to grab some things if I'll be staying at your place."

"Wait, a damn minute. I didn't agree with that."

twenty-eight

MADISON

"WELL, I agree with Massimo, Catarina. Donny needs to be with you all the time until they can figure out what's going on," I said, trying to maintain a calm tone despite the tension in the room.

"Of course, you'd say that, Madison. You're fucking my brother," Catarina barked, her voice dripping with sarcasm.

Massimo grunted, ready to defend me, but I put my hand up to stop him. "Yes, and he does thoroughly, but that has nothing to do with your safety," I replied, injecting a bit of sarcasm to defuse the tension.

The men in the room stifled their chuckles as I stepped closer to Catarina, trying to show her I understood her frustration. "We only want you safe. At least you know Donny. I wouldn't want someone I didn't know staying with me or following me around."

Catarina's face softened, and she sighed. "I'm sorry, I shouldn't have said that. I'm just frustrated. My life is supposed to be my own." She looked down, her voice cracking slightly. "If Antonio were here, he'd agree with me."

"Wait." I glanced back at Massimo, a sudden realization hitting me. "Where is Antonio? He should have been here by now."

Everyone shared a concerned glance. "Has anyone heard from him?" I asked, a knot of worry forming in my stomach.

Massimo pulled his phone out and pressed it to his ear. "It's going to voicemail," he said, his brow furrowing.

"I'm sure it's fine. He's probably tied up with the police offi-cer." Catarina sighed, though her voice betrayed her unease. "They were pissed that I left the scene."

"You're right." Massimo turned his attention back to Cata-rina. "Cat… we just need to make sure you can keep living your life on your terms." He pulled her into a hug. "Now, go with Donny."

"Thanks, Massimo. Madison, I'll call you later." Catarina gave me a half-hearted smile.

"Yes, please. I've set a date, so we should talk about your role." Hugging her quickly, I watched as the door shut. This was going to be a long road, but I knew the danger when I gave my heart to Massimo. "I'm starved. I think I'll leave you men to shop talk. Vincenzo, do you have something I can heat up?"

Heat up?" He snatched my hand, his eyes wide with mock horror. "Come, they can get started without me. I cannot let you reheat food. I'll whip up something to eat for everyone."

I smiled at Vincenzo's theatrics. "You may replace Antonio as my favorite brother if you keep feeding me like this."

"Shut your mouth. You know Antonio will always be your favorite. I'm only good for food. He's the all-around brother. Come on, Maddie, watch me cook so you can learn something."

Flipping him the finger, I held my hand out to Massimo, who hurried to catch up and lace his fingers with mine. Vincenzo was acting strangely, and I worried about him more each day that passed since the situation started back in Italy.

"Hey, Vin, are you okay?" I glanced over at Massimo, who only shrugged.

"Not really, but I will be. This whole mess opens up some darkness for me… Darkness I've spent the last three years trying to bury," Vincenzo admitted, his voice low.

"We're here for you. Don't shut us out." I said, smiling warmly. "Besides, we've set a date, and you need to find someone to be your plus one."

"That's wonderful news." He paused, placing his hand on my cheek. "But I will never have what Massimo has found in you."

"Don't say that, fratello," Massimo clapped his hand on his shoulder. "You'll find your soulmate when you least expect it. When you do, nothing else will matter. Now, I thought you promised food. Miguel will be here in an hour, and I want to have that discussion on a full belly."

"Of course, follow me," Vincenzo said, heading off toward the kitchen ahead of us.

"Does he really believe he'll never find love?" I glanced at the empty hallway.

"Yes. Vin seems to think his past transgressions marred him for a good life. He's tried to bury that part of him when all he needs to do is embrace it," Massimo said, shaking his head. "But you can't make that stubborn ass see reason."

"You're one to talk." I cocked an eyebrow at my future husband, the king of stubbornness himself.

"Um… I think Vin needs my help," Massimo hurried us down the hallway.

"That was smooth."

"Well, it's true. Both he and Antonio are trying to bury demons. One day, they're going to meet someone who defies all logic, and then," he pulled me against him, "they'll be set free."

"Is that what I did for you? Set you free?"

"More than you'll ever know, bella. Before you, I was convinced I wouldn't find someone strong enough to complete me. Then you walked into my office, and all my senses went out the door. You're the air I breathe. The stars in my sky. Without you, I am nothing."

"Keep talking like that, and we won't make it to the kitchen."

Massimo growled, capturing my lips. "You are my every-thing. I love you," he murmured against my mouth.

"And I love you. Let's go help him because I'm hungry."

Massimo swatted my butt as I walked ahead of him. "Fine, but I want dessert later."

This wasn't going to be an easy relationship, but I knew Massimo would have my back, no matter what. I had to be strong, not only for him but for the others I now considered my family.

Together, we would protect what was ours.

Together, we would be unstoppable.

epilogue

VINCENZO

I SAT across listening to Riley Lawson drone on about her qualifications and why she'd be a good fit for my restaurant —but all I could think about was the shit storm that was my life. I wanted to cancel the damn interview, but Massimo insisted it needed to be done. The woman had a confused expression when everyone scattered from the restaurant.

My eyes focused, and I realized she'd been talking. "What did you say?"

"I said I could start as soon as you needed me to." She smiled as her head cocked in question. "Is everything ok? I mean, I couldn't help but notice you were having some kind of meeting when I got here and that they all just got up and left."

I waved my hand in the air, "It's fine." I pushed to a stand and started toward the kitchen. " Follow me," I bark, not waiting to see if she does.

I'm quite surprised when she bumps into my backside when I

come to a sudden halt. Seems she can follow directions after all. I wave my arm out in front of me, "This is the kitchen."

Riley stepped around me, "Wow—this is not what I was expecting."

"Why? Did you think it was going to be like the Chili's down the street?" My tone is less than amusing as I cut my eyes to her athletic frame. She's a half foot shorter than me, making it so she has to crane her neck to look at me.

"Um… no, sir."

Hearing the word *sir* on her lips made my cock stir, but I quickly shoved it aside. This woman was the only candidate that had come close to meeting my expectations—fucking her would only create problems later.

"Your background says you worked for a private residence–as their chef. What makes you think you can handle the grueling work I expect here with the fast pace."

I let my gaze drift down her body, letting myself linger on her legs. She was dressed in a black form-fitting dress that stopped just above her knees. I didn't usually find knees sexy, but on this woman, I was rethinking my fetishes. Continuing my perusal, I nearly groaned at the sight of her shapely calves that were made to wrap around my body as I drove into her. The sound of her clearing her voice reminded me that this was an interview for my assistant, not my submissive.

The vibration of my cell phone pulled me from my dirty fantasy of her strapped down to a bed as I flogged her. Tugging my phone out, I blinked; a cryptic message from my brother demanding my presence at the casino had the hair on the nape of my neck tingling.

"Mr. Anastasi?" her voice seemed distant. "I can come in and do a trial run if that suits you."

I snapped my gaze at her, "Fine." I mindlessly walked toward the entrance, motioning to the door, "Be here tomorrow." I said, "I've got to handle a family matter."

I vaguely heard her grumble as I moved swiftly through the back and shoved out into the alley behind The Sapphire Dagger in search of my motorcycle. I slid my leg over the leather seat and hit the call button as I fumbled for my keys inside my pocket.

"Vincenzo." Massimo's voice cracked with emotion.

"What the hell is going on, Massimo—what's so important that I need to come *right* this minute? I was in the middle of the interview you insisted I hold."

"He's gone, Vin."

I slipped the key into the ignition and paused. "Who's gone?" My heart thundered inside my chest because, deep down, I knew what he was about to say.

"Antonio is missing."

I cranked the engine, "I'm on my way." Disconnecting, I slipped the device into my pocket and tugged on my helmet.

God help the world… because a fury, unlike the world, had ever seen was about to reign down on Vegas. Family was everything, and I would do anything for them.

Even if it meant unleashing the monster inside.

———

Do you believe in Monsters?

Grab book two and find out what happens when the Monsters come out to play… because not everything that happens in Vegas… stays hidden.

Grab book two to find out what happens when the monsters don't stay hidden, and secrets are exposed.

playlist

Familia *(Nicki Minaj, Anuel Aa)*

Crazy in Love *(Beyonce)*

Gimme Shelter *(The Rolling Stones)*

Sunshine of your Love *(Cream)*

House of the Rising Sun *(The Animals)*

Heathens *(Twenty One Pilots)*

White Room *(Cream)*

All Along the Watchtower *(Jimi Hendrix)*

Love me like you do *(Ellie Goulding)*

Under Your Spell *(Desire)*

Dirty Deeds Done Dirt Cheap *(AC/DC)*

Hard for Me *(Michele Morrone)*

Can't You See *(The Marshall Tucker Band)*

Listen Here on Spotify

pulitano / anastasi family history

While the characters in this story are entirely fictional, their names are not. The majority of the character names came from my family tree. Of course, I took some liberties and altered how names were paired. Vincenzo Pulitano was my great-great-grandfather, and his history inspired the Anastasi Family Syndicate family names.

Vincenzo Mario Pulitano was born in 1882 in Bovalino, Reggio di Calabria, Calabria, Italy. He immigrated to Massachusetts, USA, around 1903. He met and married his wife, Celestina Anastasi, in Boston. They had five children, including a son who died shortly after birth. One of the five was my grandmother, Annette Pulitano.

After coming to the US, Vincenzo went by the Americanized version of his name, which is found in later American records as "Vincent." He was a barber and owned his shop until he lost his business during the Great Depression.

Two of Vincent's brothers, Michele and Carlo, also immigrated to Boston, where they later married._He likely had other siblings. Notes from a granddaughter also mention two brothers and a sister, unnamed. The occupations of the brothers in her notes are "priest" and "schoolmaster"; however, the two brothers found in the records for the City of Boston are both married.

Vincent died about Mar 1949 in Medfield and was buried at St. Michael's Cemetery in Boston, Massachusetts.

This information is readily available on my family Wiki Tree.

Check out more https://www.wikitree.com/wiki/Pulitano-5

about dori

"Love, Loyalty, and the Occasional Gunshot."

Dori Pulitano, a USA Today Bestselling Author, is the naughtier, much dirtier half of Author LC Taylor. Writing men in shades of grey, the bad girl Dori embraces her Italian side with heroic hitmen, decadent conflicted dons, and oh-so-f*ckable assassins trying to trade their devilish ways for salvation —and the perfect woman to tie to their bed.

And F**k following the rules... this author is most definitely trigger-happy.

Visit www.AuthorDoriPulitano.com to learn more.

facebook.com/AlphaBookBoyfriend
instagram.com/alphabookboyfriends
tiktok.com/@alphabookboyfriend
bookbub.com/authors/dori-pulitano